BLAZE OF GLORY

Upton's cheeks darkened with anger. "People never appreciated the risks I took or gave me my just due! I *tamed* towns, Marshal Long. I stood in the middle of a dirty main street and faced gunfighters! And I killed them! I never ran nor was I beaten or humiliated."

"Congratulations," Longarm replied, "it's a shame that you never received the glory you have always desired. But few of us do. What's important now, however, is that you seem to believe that capturing the train robbers is your last chance to grab the golden ring."

"I'm older than you and I'm fast running out of time."

"Upton, I know you won't do it, but you should retire *today*," Longarm told the railroad detective. "Save yourself a lot of misery and possibly even your life."

"I can't quit! I have very little savings and I have not yet fulfilled my destiny."

Longarm had heard enough. This man was driven by delusions of grandeur and consumed by demons formed from his earliest years. Longarm started to excuse himself when Upton suddenly drew his pistol and shoved it into Longarm's belly . . .

—◄ TABOR EVANS ►—

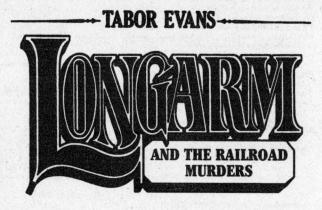

LONGARM

AND THE RAILROAD MURDERS

JOVE BOOKS, NEW YORK

THE BERKLEY PUBLISHING GROUP
Published by the Penguin Group
Penguin Group (USA) Inc.
375 Hudson Street, New York, New York 10014, USA
Penguin Group (Canada), 90 Eglinton Avenue East, Suite 700, Toronto, Ontario M4P 2Y3, Canada
(a division of Pearson Penguin Canada Inc.)
Penguin Books Ltd., 80 Strand, London WC2R 0RL, England
Penguin Group Ireland, 25 St. Stephen's Green, Dublin 2, Ireland (a division of Penguin Books Ltd.)
Penguin Group (Australia), 250 Camberwell Road, Camberwell, Victoria 3124, Australia
(a division of Pearson Australia Group Pty. Ltd.)
Penguin Books India Pvt. Ltd., 11 Community Centre, Panchsheel Park, New Delhi—110 017, India
Penguin Group (NZ), Cnr. Airborne and Rosedale Roads, Albany, Auckland 1310, New Zealand
(a division of Pearson New Zealand Ltd.)
Penguin Books (South Africa) (Pty.) Ltd., 24 Sturdee Avenue, Rosebank, Johannesburg 2196,
South Africa

Penguin Books Ltd., Registered Offices: 80 Strand, London WC2R 0RL, England

LONGARM AND THE RAILROAD MURDERS

A Jove Book / published by arrangement with the author

PRINTING HISTORY
Jove edition / March 2006

Copyright © 2006 by The Berkley Publishing Group

ISBN: 0-515-14091-0

JOVE®
Jove Books are published by The Berkley Publishing Group,
a division of Penguin Group (USA) Inc.,
375 Hudson Street, New York, New York 10014.
JOVE is a registered trademark of Penguin Group (USA) Inc.
The "J" design is a trademark belonging to Penguin Group (USA) Inc.

PRINTED IN THE UNITED STATES OF AMERICA

10 9 8 7 6 5 4 3 2 1

Chapter 1

It was April in Denver and a cold, hard rain was falling when United States Deputy Marshal Custis Long left his downtown apartment and headed for the Federal Building located near the Denver Mint. He was wearing a gray canvas raincoat over his brown suit and his flat-brimmed Stetson effectively sheeted the water from his rugged face. A tall, impressive figure in his mid-thirties, the few male pedestrians making their way along the sidewalks stepped aside without his asking. However, each time Longarm came abreast of a woman, he nodded his head in respect because he had been raised in the South and had been taught the manners of a Southern gentleman.

He had a meeting this morning at the office with his boss and friend, Marshal Billy Vail and the subject of the meeting was not a secret. Someone was systematically robbing trains and stealing huge amounts of gold, cash and United States Government Bonds. As if that weren't serious enough, the cutthroat gang of thieves had already shot eight railroad guards and pistol-whipped several others so severely that they had suffered permanent brain damage. Custis Long did not yet know the details of the robberies, but he expected to learn them this bitter morning. All he knew for certain was that the train robbers were smart and operated over a vast expanse of the West wherever the rails were carrying passengers and freight. Sometimes they would strike in Colorado, but other times in Wyoming, Utah and Nevada. Given that fact alone, Longarm figured that the thieves were riding the rails posing as innocent passengers. Most likely they were also using disguises.

At a busy street corner on Colfax Avenue the rain began to fall even harder and Longarm was loath to stand and wait for the traffic because he was getting completely soaked. There were three other individuals waiting to cross the intersection and they looked as miserable as Longarm was feeling. Damned rain! It had been coming down in buckets for nearly a week and Cherry Creek was overflowing and causing a great deal of destruction and consternation among the city dwellers near its raging waters.

Longarm also knew that it had been an especially hard winter up in the Rocky Mountains and those towns at higher elevations like Central City, Evergreen and Cripple Creek would be a quagmire with roads clogged with mud. They would be impassible and filled with stranded freight wagons mired to their hubs. Mule skinners, never a quiet bunch, would be cursing a blue streak. At least, Longarm thought, he did not have to suffer the mud or venture down into some flooded silver or gold mine and try to earn his daily bread.

"Excuse me, sir? Could you *please* help me get across this washed out street? I'm shivering with cold, in a terrible hurry, and I just can't stand here getting drenched and waiting any longer."

Longarm turned to see a young woman who would have been attractive had she not appeared already half drowned. The desperate lady was about to throw herself recklessly into the busy intersection filled with wagons and carriages which were all moving with haste in an attempt to get out of the harsh elements.

"I'll do what I can," he vowed. "Take my hand and we'll try to get across without getting trampled."

The woman offered him the barest hint of a smile to show her gratitude and took Longarm's big paw saying, "I've been standing here waiting to cross for at least five minutes and I'm soaked through and through and chilled to my very bones."

"I'm sorry," Longarm said, eyeing the swift water running across Colfax from curb to curb. "The water is swift and at least a foot deep."

"Yes, I know."

Longarm thought a moment, then said, "Miss, if you don't mind, I think it best that I carried you to the other side. Otherwise . . ."

Longarm did not finish because he did not want to seem forward, but the water was very swift and muddy and he feared the young woman would fall and get completely soaked.

She only considered his offer for a second, then said, "You are very kind, sir. But I'll manage to cross by holding your hand."

Longarm turned to the other pair waiting. "Are you coming with us?"

They shook their heads and turned to walk away.

"Let's go then," Longarm told the young woman as he stepped into the current that immediately surged over the tops of his boots filling them with freezing water.

The woman staggered when she left the sidewalk, but she was game and plunged ahead with a near death grip on Longarm's hand. They were doing fairly well getting across Colfax until a wagon filled with garbage refused to slow down and give them clear passage. In fact, the two bearded and burly men huddled on the seat shouted a curse at Longarm. To add salt to the wound, the driver used his whip on his poor horses to drive them forward even faster.

Longarm and the lady would have been struck by the wagon had he not pulled up suddenly. Even so, the wheel horse banged Longarm with its heavy shoulder knocking both him and the woman down in the middle of the flooded street. Longarm shouted at the two men and heard their coarse laughter in response. He noted a faded sign on the wagon that read, GANTRY'S GARBAGE COMPANY.

"Are you all right, miss?" Longarm said, scooping the woman up from the flood and surging ahead. "I'm so sorry that I fell."

"It wasn't your fault, sir. It was those awful men in the garbage wagon! They almost ran us over. We could have been killed just now."

When he safely reached the other side of the street Longarm deposited the lady on the sidewalk. He was completely soaked and madder than hell. "I'm going to look that pair up," he told her. "Do you have any more streets to cross this morning?"

"Thankfully not. I'm going into the Mint to apply for a job as a secretary." She shook her head and stared down at her coat and the bottom of her wet and ruined dress. "Or at least, that was my original intention."

"I work in that Federal Building next door," he said. "Perhaps our paths will cross again."

"I hope under drier and happier circumstances," she

said. "I don't know how I'll win a job looking this morning like I tried to mop up Colfax Avenue with myself. I doubt it's even worth my time going in for the interview."

"You have nothing to lose by trying," Longarm said, trying to offer some encouragement. "Just tell whoever is interviewing you that you fell in the street, but wanted the job so badly that not even a river of water and a garbage wagon could stop you."

She canted her head back and smiled. "Do you really think that I might still have a chance even looking like I'm a drowned rat?"

He could tell that she desperately needed some assurance. Her hair was probably blonde but it was plastered across her face and dark. But even so, he could tell that she was pretty. She had a heart-shaped face, blue eyes and full lips. Of medium height, he guessed her to be in her twenties.

"Tell them that United States Marshal Custis Long recommends that you be hired because only a determined and brave woman would have come out in weather like this to interview for their job."

"Do you know anyone at the personnel office there?" she asked.

"No. But they might know me," he said with a good natured shrug of his broad shoulders. "I have something of a reputation in Denver. Try it. Can't hurt."

"I will," she replied.

She looked at him for a moment through the pouring rain and then she surprised him by lifting up on her toes and kissing his cheek. "It's not often that a man sweeps me off my feet and acts so gallantly."

Longarm said nothing.

"My name is Miss Milly Cannon. And I do thank you

5

with all my heart . . . even if I'm turned away from the interview without a word of encouragement."

He tipped his hat. "I wish you well, Miss Cannon."

She started to leave but them turned suddenly and came back for a moment. "Marshal, please don't feel obligated on my account to even the score with the driver of that garbage wagon and his companion. With the rain falling as hard as it is, he might just not have seen us out there trying to cross Colfax."

"Oh," Longarm said, his expression darkening, "he saw us all right. And he could have reined those horses just a little to the side and missed us. Or better yet, have pulled them up for a moment or two so we could cross. What he did was mean and spiteful."

"Yes, but he didn't actually break the law, did he?"

"He did in my book," Longarm said, his anger very near the surface. "We could have been run over and killed. So I'll go have a word with that driver, of that you can be certain."

"Thanks again, Marshal Long."

She turned and hurried off to the Mint for her interview. Longarm hesitated in the driving rain to watch her bound up the stone stairs in front of the building. She was graceful and he liked what she looked like from the back side.

He just stood in the rain watching until Milly Cannon disappeared. Then, he hesitated, trying to decide if he should go directly to Gantry's Garbage and have his words with the driver and his companion, or first go to his scheduled office meeting with Billy Vail.

"I'd better go to the office first," he muttered. "No use in getting into more trouble than necessary on this wet and miserable morning. But I'll find those boys later and I'll make sure that they are taught a lesson."

His decision made, Longarm went striding off to the Federal Building, dripping muddy streams of water in the marble floored foyer. Billy Vail would be appalled at his bedraggled appearance as would the others who saw him enter the building. But Longarm did not care. Most likely, his being soaked would insure that the meeting would be a short one. And that was all to the good because, if there was anything that Longarm loathed it was long office meetings.

Chapter 2

When Longarm stepped into Billy Vail's office, there were three well dressed men waiting. The moment that they saw Longarm they stopped talking and stared.

"What the hell happened to you?" Billy finally asked. "Did you slip and fall into Cherry Creek on the way over here this morning?"

Longarm had already shucked off his raincoat and Stetson but his suit was still as wet as a dishrag. "I was nearly run over by a damned garbage wagon when I tried helping a young lady cross the street outside. But never mind that. What's going on?"

Billy rose from behind his desk and introduced his visitors. "This is Detective Otis Upton," he said motioning to a tall, thin man about forty with a handlebar mustache and pale eyes, "and Detective Jason Baxter. They work for the Union Pacific Railroad and have been on the case I already mentioned for about four months."

Baxter stepped forward first. He was in his late twenties, short but powerfully built with a bull neck and sloping shoulders. He wore a full beard and a genuinely warm smile. "Pleased to meet you, Marshal Long. We've heard a lot about you over the years."

Longarm shook Baxter's hand and then that of the older detective who did not seem nearly so friendly. In fact, Upton's expression was so sour he appeared to have just bitten into a lemon. Or perhaps, Longarm thought, the railroad man was unhappy to be having a meeting with federal officers. There was, unfortunately, very often a dose of professional jealousy between law agencies. And from Upton's expression, Longarm immediately sensed that this meeting was not of his choosing.

"Gentleman, would you like coffee this morning?" Billy asked.

Feeling wet and chilled, Longarm would have preferred a double shot of Three X brandy but Billy would not have approved so he reluctantly settled for coffee. Detective Baxter and Upton passed on the coffee which was probably wise because Billy's secretary made the absolute worst in Denver.

"Now," Billy said, "let's begin this meeting." He gave the two railroad detectives an encouraging smile. "I know that it's never easy for professionals like ourselves to seek outside help, but sometimes it's necessary."

"I *didn't* seek your help," Upton snapped. "I'm here because the Union Pacific said I have to come. And the truth is that I've got a handle on this gang of thieves and murderers." He held up his hand, thumb and forefinger close together. "I'm *this* close to capturing those bastards."

"Is that right?" Billy said without a hint of skepticism.

"That's right," Upton replied, vigorously nodding his head. "I've taught Jason here a thing or two and he can second my feelings about not wanting any interference in our company business."

"I see." Billy leaned back in his office chair and steepled his pudgy fingers. Longarm had to admire his boss's self-restraint. It was clear that Detective Upton was riled about this meeting and didn't want any help in the case. It was less clear that Detective Baxter felt the same professional jealousy. But what was obvious was that Billy was going to try to be diplomatic and not ruffle any feathers unless it was necessary.

"The thing of it is, Marshal Vail," the younger railroad detective said, "we're sitting here in Denver when we should be out on the rails trying to nail those guys to a wall. Why, they could be robbing one of our trains this very moment while we waste time talking."

" 'Waste time?' " Billy inquired, a slight touch of sarcasm in his voice. "Is *that* what you think we are doing this morning, Detective Baxter?"

The young man shifted uncomfortably in his chair. "Well, I didn't exactly mean to say that," he hedged.

"What did you mean to say?"

"It's just that we nearly caught the gang the third time that they struck the payroll coach. It was about a month ago about ten miles west of Rock Springs. We couldn't have missed the gang by more than an hour." Baxter shook his head. "Just one darned hour!"

"But you *did* miss them," Billy said, cutting the two detectives not one bit of slack. "And now do you know even which state or territory they might be hiding in?"

"We think Utah," Baxter said, not sounding very confident of that prediction. "Our best guess is that they're holing up somewhere around the Great Salt Lake."

Longarm was almost impressed. "That's a lot of country, Detective Baxter. What makes you think so?"

"They've struck the Union Pacific three times within fifty miles of Salt Lake. Then they just vanish into the brush and alkali flats."

Longarm nodded. "I see. How many times have they robbed your trains in Wyoming and Nevada?"

Upton interrupted. "Twice each. But . . ."

Longarm cut the older man off in mid-sentence. "And California?"

"Not once," Baxter admitted.

Longarm thought about that a moment then asked, "How many men do you think are involved with this gang?"

The two railroad detectives exchanged glances and it was Upton who spoke. "It's hard to say," he began. "In several of the train robberies, there were no more than five. But in one or two others, witnesses say there were at least seven . . . possibly eight."

"How do they do it?" Billy asked.

"They buy passenger tickets," Upton answered, his face red with anger. "They buy first class and coach. They sit apart from each other and when they reach a spot where they've decided to rob our trains, they pull guns and go about their unlawful business."

Longarm said, "And I understand they are not in the least bit concerned about murdering your employees when they are confronted."

Upton nodded in agreement. "That's right. We've lost a few good employees who refused to do as they were ordered by the outlaws. And two passengers thought they'd be heroes and drew their guns. It caused a riot and needless wholesale bloodshed. Three passengers died, including the pair of foolish would-be heroes."

Longarm's brows knit with concern. "And I expect those deaths are causing your passenger count to fall faster than a stone."

"Yes," Detective Baxter quickly agreed. "The Union Pacific's passenger counts are falling dramatically. We're losing a great deal of revenue besides the money and valuables being stolen."

Baxter steepled his short fingers together and leaned forward. "What we have, Marshal Long, is a serious, serious situation and rising panic among both passengers and our railroad crews."

"It would seem so," Longarm said.

Billy reached for his pipe and pouch of tobacco. "Has anyone seen the faces of these outlaws?"

"Not exactly," Detective Upton said bitterly.

"What does *that* mean?"

"They wear disguises when they board as passengers. Wigs. Clothes to make them look like bankers or cowboys. Fake mustaches. The truth of the matter is that we can't get accurate descriptions. Everyone thinks they know what the outlaw in their coach looked like. But their descriptions conflict with each other. And they rarely match the descriptions given to us by the passengers that witnessed previous train robberies."

"I see," Billy replied, carefully packing his pipe with an expensive brand of Turkish tobacco that was so strong it could kill mosquitoes and flies at twenty feet. "So this makes identification extremely difficult."

"Yeah," Upton growled, "but we're starting to see similarities. For example, one guy is huge. Must stand six-seven. Big lantern jaw and bad teeth. Those things can't be disguised. Another one is his opposite. Short. No taller than Jason here."

"I'm not *that* short," Detective Baxter objected with indignation. "I'm five-foot-eight and that's just about average. In boots, I'm even taller than average, dammit."

Upton let the objection stand and it was clear to Longarm that the younger detective was self-conscious about his height. That was probably why he had worked to build up his obviously powerful physique. Jason's nose was crooked and Longarm saw that several of his knuckles had been broken, confirming that the younger detective was not afraid to mix it up with his fists when insulted by taller men. Longarm understood and accepted that fact. Small men often had to be tougher than big men, if they rebelled at being teased or bullied all their lives. As children, they had to learn to scrap and they were often tougher than boot leather.

"Jason," Longarm said, "how long have you been with the Union Pacific?"

"About four years. I started out shoveling coal in the tender then caught a break and saved one of the railroad bigwigs from a saloon beating in Cheyenne. He gave me a chance at being a detective."

"Good," Longarm said. "And I'm sure that Otis here is teaching you well."

Longarm turned to the older detective. "I'd guess you were a marshal in some town along the tracks. Is that right?"

"As a matter of fact I was," Upton said proudly. "I was the marshal of three railroad towns. But they all went belly up and I finally got smart and got a job with the Union Pacific. I know my job, Long. I know that I can catch those thieves and murderers . . . if left to my own devices."

"I'm sure that's true," Longarm agreed. "But it seems that we are going to have to work together. Your bosses have obviously made that clear and my boss, Marshal Vail, feels the same way."

Billy lit his pipe and nodded in silent but firm agreement. "I have no doubt that, if you put your heads together, you can do more to save lives and property. Deputy Marshal Custis Long is my best man. I've got two others that . . ."

"No!" Upton lowered his voice. "I won't tolerate a crowd of feds stumbling all over the case. *One man.* Marshal Long here, if he's your best. But no more. And there's another thing."

Longarm could guess what was coming next and he wasn't wrong.

"The other thing is," Upton added, eyes squinting as they shifted from Longarm to Billy and back to Longarm, "I give the orders and Marshal Long follows them to the letter."

"No," Longarm said, turning to stare at his boss. "I won't do that under *any* circumstances."

Billy puffed on his pipe and he considered this impasse. On one side was his best deputy who had always worked independent of supervision. On the other side was the pair of Union Pacific Railroad detectives who didn't even want to be here in the first place. What should he do?

Billy forced a smile and turned it on the railroad men. "Detectives," he began, "I appreciate your sentiments and respect your ability. However, I'm afraid that I have to go with a decision that Marshal Custis Long will answer to no one except me."

Detective Upton jumped out of his chair. "I figured you'd say that. Jason, didn't I tell you they wouldn't agree to work under us?"

The younger detective gave a slight nod of his head. "Yes, you did."

Upton stabbed a finger at Billy. "Sir, this meeting is over. We will return to our duties and I have no doubt that we will catch this gang and send them either to the gallows or to a federal prison."

Upton put on his hat and started to turn for the door.

"Hold it up a moment," Billy ordered.

Upton turned. "What now?"

Billy's eyes bored into the senior railroad detective. "Upton," he began, "you don't seem to understand that I have been in communication with the *vice president* of your Union Pacific Railroad and he has given me explicit instructions stating that our help is vital and that we will work completely under our authority."

Upton slowly absorbed this information, face darkening with anger. Finally, he managed to blurt, "Do you have any written proof of what you say?"

"As a matter of fact, I do," Billy Vail told the senior railroad detective. He reached into his coat pocket and produced a telegram. "I think this ought to be quite convincing."

Upton snatched the telegram from Billy's hand, read it quickly and then dropped it on the desk. He was so angry that his jaw muscles were corded and he ground his teeth in order to stifle an outburst. While this was happening, Jason Baxter picked up and also read the telegram.

"Well," young Baxter said, "that seems clear enough. So your deputy marshal will work independently and he is to be given our full cooperation and assistance."

"That's right," Billy said. "However, if you two aren't prepared to offer that assistance in good faith . . . then I'm

sure I can get your vice president to make other arrange-
ments. Perhaps with other railroad detectives."

"No!" Upton lowered his voice. "We'll cooperate."

"In good faith and in full measure?" Billy pointedly
asked.

"Yes, dammit!"

Billy turned to Longarm. "How do you want to handle
this?"

Longarm had been thinking about that very question
and now he answered, "I don't think it serves any purpose
for me to work side by side with these detectives. Rather, I
feel that we should work independently on different parts
of the railroad, but keep regular communication."

"And how on earth would that happen?" Upton asked,
not bothering to hide his skepticism.

"It wouldn't be that difficult," Longarm explained. "We
can prearrange our communications through the telegraph
offices. Use a code word to identify ourselves and a few
code words to convey whatever new information we have
obtained."

"It sounds way too complicated," Upton argued.

"Trust me," Longarm told the two railroad detectives,
"it will work. Also, I would prefer that I not be known as a
federal marshal. I will pose as a . . . businessman, rancher
or perhaps even a gambler. I've done that many times before and it's worked very much in my favor."

"Do what you want," Upton told him. "But just don't get
in our way of making an arrest."

Longarm didn't like this man and he dropped all pre-
tense of civility toward Upton. "I'll not get in your way and
ask only that you railroad dicks stay out of my way."

Billy Vail sighed, probably because it was now clear

that Longarm and the two detectives would not really be cooperating at all. But, he had suspected that would be the case from the very beginning of the meeting.

"Gentlemen," he said, "I suggest that this meeting is over. Why don't the three of you meet this afternoon . . . when Custis has had a chance to change his suit and take a bath . . . and then hammer out the details. I would say only one thing before I end this meeting and that is that your best chance of stopping this ruthless railroad gang is to work well together. Both innocent passengers and crew on the Union Pacific are being killed, robbed and wounded. Government money as well as private money is fast disappearing. We need to put a stop to this as quickly as possible. Is that agreed all around?"

Longarm nodded. The two railroad detectives nodded.

"Then, gentlemen," Billy said, finally smiling around the stem of his pipe, "shake hands in the spirit of friendship and cooperation and good luck and good hunting!"

They shook hands and then started to leave the room. "Marshal Long," Billy said, "would you please remain for a moment?"

"Yes sir."

When the door closed, Longarm relaxed. "Thanks for standing by me, Boss. You know that I couldn't have worked under Otis Upton. The man is an overbearing ass and I don't think he's half as smart as he thinks he is."

"I agree." Billy frowned. "But his underling, Deputy Baxter, is far more open to cooperation and learning. If I were you, Custis, I'd try to work through the younger detective and around the older."

"I doubt I'll need the help of either man."

"Don't be too sure of that," Billy said. "The Union Pacific has many resources available and they are desperate to catch this gang of thieves and murderers. Use every resource available and never fall into the kind of jealousy and ignorance that we've just seen from Detective Upton."

"Yes sir."

"And for heavens sakes, go home and take a bath and get a change of clothing."

"Sure. When will I be leaving?"

"Why on the next train, of course."

"Of course. That would be tomorrow morning."

"That's right," Billy said. "And I'll be waiting for you at the train depot with cash for your trip and any last-minute instructions or information I might receive from the Union Pacific management."

Longarm dipped his head in agreement. "I'll have to get a code to those guys so we can keep in touch."

"Make it a simple one," Billy advised. "Otherwise, I doubt that it would be decipherable by Detective Otis Upton."

Longarm had to laugh at that as he went out the door.

Chapter 3

When Longarm left the Federal Building, the rain was still falling hard and the streets were overflowing with brown, swirling water. He started toward his nearby apartment then abruptly changed direction. With his head down and the brim of his hat throwing off a steady stream of water Longarm made a determined march up Colfax staying on the sidewalks when he had to, but crossing the torrent whenever it was necessary.

Gantry's Garbage Company was a rundown business located in a rough neighborhood about four blocks south of Sherman Avenue. Longarm had passed it hundreds of times and the stench of decaying rubbish had always made him walk a little faster. He knew that the business operated in the worst parts of town picking up garbage with a fleet of ugly wagons and teams of underfed mules and horses. He had heard that the founder of the company, Amos Gantry, had died and left the business to his two sons, Moses and Jasper, who were just as penny-pinching and slovenly as their deceased old man.

Now, standing at the gate of the garbage yard with the steady rain coming down Longarm could see that there was an office, a stable and perhaps half a dozen of the kinds of decrepit garbage wagons that had nearly run him and Miss Cannon down early that morning. There were also several pitiful-looking watchdogs that were huddled under a dripping porch.

Longarm set his jaw and marched into the yard. The dogs, large and mangy, jumped up and began to bark but Longarm didn't concern himself with them because they were too cowardly to come across the yard in the driving rain. Dogs that squeamish certainly ought not to offer a serious threat.

He saw no one as he passed the hundreds of garbage barrels and piles of rotting refuse. There were crows and ravens even out in this foul weather trying to eat their fill and the closer Longarm got to the office the louder the pathetic watchdogs howled.

Finally, someone came out of the office and kicked one of the dogs. It yelped and ran. Its companions shot off the porch and streaked for the protection of the company's dilapidated barn and stable.

"What do you want?" a fat, bearded man shouted at Longarm who recognized him as the one sitting beside the driver.

Longarm didn't answer but hopped up on the porch and growled, "What's your name?"

"Jasper Gantry. Who's asking?"

"Where's your brother?"

"He's inside. Now you git!"

Jasper was about six-foot tall with unruly black hair and close set eyes that radiated insult. He made the mistake of

22

trying to push Longarm off the porch and back into the rain. The mistake cost him a bellyache when Longarm drove his big fist into Jasper's big gut. The ugly garbage-man grunted and doubled up in agony. Longarm hit him a second time with a thundering right cross that landed solidly against Jasper's jaw and sent the man sprawling. Jasper grabbed a porch post to keep from spilling into the mud but Longarm kicked him in the side of the knee and sent him tumbling into a huge puddle. The man was down but not completely out. He started to drag himself back to the porch and Longarm went to stop him.

"Who the hell are you?" Jasper choked as he looked up with the rain blurring his vision.

"I'm the fella that you and your brother tried to run down this morning on Colfax. I was with that young lady and you thought knocking us over in the water was the funniest thing you'd done in a long time. Remember?"

Jasper squinted hard up at Longarm but he wasn't quick enough to save himself when Longarm's boot caught him in the throat. Jasper flopped heavily over on his back with his hands flying to his windpipe as he struggled for air. Longarm stomped him deep into the mud with his boot and then kicked him in the ear for good measure. Jasper tried to raise a hand to protect himself but Longarm was already moving back to the porch and into the office.

"What . . . who are you!" Moses demanded, rising from behind a cluttered desk with a cheap cigar in one hand and a bottle of rotgut hooch clenched in the other.

Longarm tipped back his hat and his expression was deadly. "Don't you remember? I'm the fella you drove your team of horses into this morning and knocked down. And even worse, you knocked down a young lady."

"What the hell are you doin' here!"

"You're about to find out," Longarm said as he moved across the office.

Moses was a little quicker on the uptake than his fat brother. He must have seen the look of murder in Longarm's eyes or maybe he saw the fresh blood on Longarm's knuckles. Either way, he hurled the bottle of whiskey at Longarm with both speed and accuracy. The bottle struck Longarm in the chest and momentarily slowed his advance. It was just enough time for Moses to tear open his top desk drawer and start to drag out a Colt revolver.

Longarm knew that he was a dead man if he went around the desk to get to his man so he dove straight over the top of it and caught Moses with a wild overhand right hand that knocked the man backward. Longarm landed on Moses and he felt the man trying to drag the gun up between them so that he could pull the trigger and end the fight. Longarm grabbed the man's wrist and bent it backward until Moses screamed and the gun spilled from his hand. At the same time, however, Moses had the presence of mind to drive his cigar into the side of Longarm's neck.

Flesh burned and Longarm shouted in pain and anger. He couldn't get his arm up to deliver a smashing blow to the man's face so he slammed his cocked elbow downward instead. He heard the pop of nasal bones and Moses bellowed. Longarm broke free, reared up and pounded the man with both fists so savagely that, in seconds, Moses didn't look like Moses anymore.

He dragged the beaten man to his feet and drove his knee into Moses' groin, crushing the garbageman's testicles. Then, he picked up the fallen and still-smoking cigar and jammed it into Moses' ear.

Moses screamed loud enough to be heard all the way up to Cheyenne. He fell to his knees begging for mercy, and Longarm, still furious and nearly out of control, picked a paperweight off the desk and fed it to Moses, knocking most of the man's already rotting front teeth down his throat.

"Please, no more! Please!"

"If you or your brother ever again try to run a lady down in the street . . . or a man . . . for that matter . . . I'll whip you both so badly that you won't even be able to recognize yourselves. Is that understood?"

Moses managed to nod his head a moment before he fainted.

Longarm couldn't stand the heavy, stale air in the office so he walked outside. He stood on the porch for a moment watching a badly beaten Jasper slither through the mud toward the stable.

"If I could get away with it," he muttered to himself, "I'd burn this whole stinking outfit right down to the ground and it would be good riddance for Denver," he said to himself.

Longarm lit a cheroot and tossed the match into the office hoping it might land on some papers or junk and catch fire. But it went out so he pulled the brim of his hat down close over his eyes and left Gantry's Garbage Company without a backward glance.

He was crossing back across the street on Colfax heading to his apartment when he heard someone shout his name. Longarm turned to see a still-drenched Milly Cannon hurrying after him.

"Hi," he said. "You still out in this bad weather?"

"I can't get any more soaked than I already am. And what about you? You look as wet as I do."

25

"I *am* wet," Longarm agreed, managing a smile and taking a pull on his cheroot.

"Your hand. It's bleeding!"

"It's nothing."

"But your knuckles are all chewed up," Milly persisted. Then, her eyes widened with shock. "And what happened to your poor neck?"

"Cigar," he said, not wanting to elaborate.

"Someone *burned* you?"

"Yep."

"Oh my heavens. You look terrible. You ought to see a doctor."

"No time for that," he replied. "I've got to get ready to leave town on tomorrow's train."

Milly took his arm. "If I can't get you to see a doctor, at least I can patch you up myself."

"Where are you taking me?"

"I have a little apartment close by."

Longarm decided to go along with that. "What about that secretary's job you were interviewing for at the Denver Mint?"

"I got it and I start next Monday!" Milly beamed even though she looked so drowned. "And I've you to thank for that."

"How so?"

"When Mr. Anderson interviewed me he asked what in the world happened on the way to the Mint to get me so drenched. So I told him the whole story including your name and how gallant you were to help me across Colfax. And, just like you predicted, he was impressed both with my determination to see the interview through as well as the fact that I knew you personally."

"Well," Longarm said. "I'm glad. I have had some

26

chances to help those folks out at the Mint. So it all worked out just fine."

"That's for sure! I'm even starting at a better wage than I expected. And Mr. Anderson says that I'll have an opportunity to advance on the job."

Longarm knew George Anderson. The man was a capable administrator, but a womanizer even though he had a wife and a bunch of kids. "Just watch out for him," Longarm warned the young woman. "Anderson has a roving eye and the hands to match."

Milly laughed. "I know how to protect myself from men and I'm no blushing schoolgirl," she confessed. "And as for the dapper Mr. Anderson, I believe I can handle him. If worse comes to worse, I can quit the job or wear him out chasing me around the office. I'm ten years younger and fifty pounds lighter."

"Glad to hear you've got it all figured out."

Milly frowned. "But it's *you* that I'm worried about. I've got some medicine at my place; that burn on your neck looks extremely painful."

"It is," Longarm admitted. "Over the year I've been stabbed, shot, clubbed and nearly strangled, but getting burned is one of the most painful wounds of all."

"A soothing ointment will help with the burn as well as your knuckles. And, if you're up for it, I'm going to stop at the market on our way and buy us some champagne and the makings of a good supper. It's a celebration in honor of our newfound friendship and my new job."

"Milly, I can take you out to dinner so you don't have to do that."

"Of course I don't have to. But I want to." Milly took his arm but then stopped abruptly in the rain. "Unless you're married or don't want to. . . ."

"I'm not married and I'd enjoy sharing champagne and dinner with you this evening," he told her. "But I have to pack for a trip and make a few preparations for tomorrow."

"Of course. I'll set you free by eight o'clock," she promised. "Unless, that is, you change your mind and want to stay a little later."

She had a come-on look in her eye that was very encouraging to Longarm. "Just in case you haven't already guessed, I'm easily corrupted," he said.

Milly winked. "So am I! Furthermore, I'm employed again and in the mood to celebrate."

"Sounds good."

"Yeah," she giggled, "doesn't it though."

Longarm pulled the brim of his hat down tight and smiled. "This day hasn't been all too great up until now, but I have a feeling things are going to get better fast."

"So do I." She smiled up at him. "If it's not some secret government mission, where are you going tomorrow?"

Longarm knew his answer would sound stupid or evasive, but he couldn't really help it. "To be perfectly honest, I'm not sure."

"What do you mean?"

"I'm after a gang of train robbers," he explained, seeing no harm in telling the woman the challenge he was going to be facing out on the Union Pacific Railroad line. "And they could be hiding anywhere between Cheyenne and Sacramento."

"How on earth will you possibly find them?"

"I don't know," he said, hearing the crash of thunder overhead. "But why don't we just keep moving and talk about it later?"

"Great idea."

They hurried to a little market and Milly bought the best champagne that the store had to offer. It wasn't imported from France nor was it a rare or expensive vintage, but Longarm wasn't complaining. Furthermore, Milly bought them both porterhouse steaks and greens for a salad.

"Have I forgotten anything?" she asked at the counter.

"Maybe a drop of brandy would be good to take the chill out of our bones when we get to your apartment. I'll buy it."

"Fair enough," Milly told him.

Her apartment was small but immaculate and cheery. Even better, she had left the heater on and the place was toasty warm. Longarm looked around and thought how much nicer women could fix things up than a man. His own apartment was about the same size but it looked like a rat's den most of the time. The only one besides himself who could stand it living there was a striped orange alley cat he'd named Sunny. Sunny was big and rangy and didn't give a hoot about anything except what was placed in his food dish. He never complained but seemed grateful for small favors which was why Longarm tolerated him. When he left on assignments, he paid a neighbor to crack his upstairs window so Sunny could come and go and always have a meal. As far as Longarm was concerned, as long as Sunny didn't start crapping on his bed or floor, the tomcat had a permanent home.

"I'm dripping all over your floor," Longarm said, glancing down at his feet.

"Take off your coat and boots," she told him. "Put them outside in the hallway."

"Are you sure no one will steal them?" Longarm asked.

"I wouldn't want to have to leave without them in this storm."

Milly laughed. "I'm positive." To prove it, she placed her own coat and overshoes in the hallway, then helped him off with his coat. There were hooks on the hallway walls which made things convenient.

"Now," Milly said, closing the door behind them and locking it. "Off with your wet shirt, vest and pants."

Longarm was a bit surprised by this request, but happy to oblige. His clothes were soaked. Without a word, Milly placed them all on a hanger near her little furnace saying, "They'll be dry in less than an hour."

"What about *your* wet clothes?" he asked.

"Hmmm, I guess I'd better do the same with them," Milly told him.

She went into her bedroom, not bothering to close the door, and disrobed. Longarm was a gentleman, but he was also a man and what he saw in that brief moment while she was changing looked beautiful.

"There," Milly said, hanging her wet dress and underclothes near the furnace. "I guess that everything will be warm and dry and we can enjoy our little celebration."

"You're a very lovely young woman," Longarm said, taking his bottle of brandy to the counter and opening it. "Glasses?"

"Up in the shelf."

Longarm poured two glasses of the amber liquid and gave one to Milly. "To your new job!" he said in a toast.

"And to your health and safety, Marshal Custis Long."

They drank and the brandy warmed their bodies right down to their toes.

"Now, the medication for your knuckles and that terrible burn mark on your neck," she told him.

30

Milly had long, supple fingers and a gentle touch. Longarm closed his eyes and let her do the healing work, and when he opened his eyes, Milly's face was only inches from his own.

"You have beautiful brown eyes," he told her.

"I like yours, too," she said a moment before their lips met.

Their kiss was like a spark that started a bonfire. The next thing they knew they were tearing off what little they wore and were racing for Milly's bed. Longarm pushed her down and paid earnest homage to her large, firm breasts. Milly sighed and moaned with delight. She reached down and played with his manhood until it stood as straight as a telephone pole and then Milly laid back, spread her legs and whispered, "Come on in, darling. I got a warm place waiting just for you tonight, and it isn't dry."

Longarm needed no further encouragement. He was an eager and ardent lover, but one who knew how to take his time in order to satisfy a beautiful woman. So he entered her by easing himself in and out while his lips and tongue danced lightly over Milly's hard nipples.

"Oh my," she breathed, "don't stop what you're doing. Don't stop all night long."

He began to move into her faster and deeper as his mouth closed over her breasts, sucking and licking. Milly wrapped her long legs around his waist and begin to kiss his hair and thrust her hips up to meet his powerful thrusts.

"Oh, Marshal! Oh that's so nice!"

Longarm thought it was far better than nice and the harder he pumped and sucked the wilder this woman became. He went after her for a good fifteen minutes until they were both drenched with sweat and half out of their minds with passion.

"I can't hold back any longer," he grunted.

"Me neither! Do it, Marshal! Do it now!"

Longarm was ready and just as he began to pump his seed into her body, Milly's back arched and she screamed with her legs locking behind his back like the jaws of a vise as they both lost themselves in the incredible throes of intense carnal pleasure.

Afterward, they lay back gasping for air and staring up at the ceiling. Finally, Milly rolled over on her side facing him and whispered, "You are one fine loverman."

"And you're a helluva lot of woman," he replied with a wide grin of appreciation. "And what about those steaks and that champagne?"

She giggled. "I was thinking we could just eat each other and wouldn't want a thing more."

Longarm enjoyed her joke. But, the truth of it was, he felt famished. And he knew that he needed red meat to keep up his strength for what was beginning to shape up as a marathon night of intense coupling.

"All right," she said. "I'll get up, pour us some bubbly and then start cooking."

"We can take a few breaks along the way, can't we?" he asked.

Milly kissed him tenderly. "Marshal Long," she breathed, "I'm going to have you for *dessert*!"

Longarm thought that sounded just about right. He got up and helped Milly set her little table and then they sampled the wine. All in all, he thought, he couldn't have imagined a finer send-off on what was probably going to be a damned dangerous railroad assignment somewhere out in the big country.

In the small hours of the next morning, when Longarm was dressing and preparing to go back to his own apartment and feed his alley cat and pack for a trip that might last weeks or even months, he left Milly asleep but with a note on her bedroom dresser that read: *Good luck with your new job. See you when I get back. Keep dry and keep smiling. Custis.*

Chapter 4

The Denver Pacific Railroad stretched straight as a string north for 106 miles until it bumped into the Union Pacific line at Cheyenne. It was a short line railroad but a busy and profitable one with a daily departure at 9:23 a.m. and a daily arrival at 5:45 p.m. and the train was usually filled going in both directions.

Now, five minutes before departure, Longarm showed up at the train station looking as if he'd just been pulled sideways through a small, jagged knot hole. After leaving Milly, he had gone home to get a few hours of sleep and had awakened much too late to make his normal trip preparations. So he'd leaped out of bed, hurriedly dressed, packed and then had hailed a carriage down to catch the northbound.

"Dammit, I've been waiting here for the last forty-five minutes!" Billy Vail shouted as Longarm ran up to board. "What happened to you? You look as if you've been out all night on a bender."

"Nope," Longarm said, "as a matter of fact, I was in bed quite early and didn't leave it until this morning."

"*Whose* bed?"

"Never you mind," Longarm told his angry boss.

"Custis, you didn't even shave and you smell like . . ." Billy had an exceptionally keen sense of smell and now he leaned in on Longarm and inhaled two or three times quickly. "You smell like a musk ox."

Despite the situation, Longarm had to laugh out loud. "And how would you know what a musk ox smelled like?"

"Well," Billy snorted, "if you can stand the truth, you really smell like the butt end of a . . . never mind. Are you prepared for this assignment?"

"Sure. Got any new information from the Union Pacific brass?"

"Only that the gang you're after just hit another of their trains about thirty miles west of Elko, Nevada. Killed two guards and wounded three passengers . . . one of which is not expected to survive. Got away with some of the railroad's payroll as well as some government money."

"How did they do it this time?"

"Same as always, I suppose." Billy shook his head. "I didn't get any particulars. Apparently, the marshal in Elko formed a posse and went after the gang. Maybe they'll catch them, but I have my doubts because there is so much rough, dry country out there to search. You could hide an army of thousands in that desert and they'd never be found."

"That's true enough," Longarm agreed. "And those Ruby Mountains west of Elko are damned near impossible to cover. Lots of dead end canyons and very little water to be found unless you have a Paiute Indian guide or know exactly where to look."

"Custis, did you know that the Union Pacific is offering a five thousand dollar reward for information leading to the capture of that bunch?"

"No," Longarm said, not one bit pleased to hear this news. "But that much money ought to bring out plenty of hungry bounty hunters and lawmen. But all those hunters will just muddy the waters for me."

"Probably." Billy started to say more but then the train's locomotive blasted its steam whistle and anyone still standing on the loading platform began to clamber onboard.

"Look," Billy said, handing Longarm a brown envelope which he knew would be filled with cash. "There's three hundred dollars for travel and expenses. Use it wisely for a change."

"Might not be enough to hold me over long enough to do the job," Longarm said, slipping the envelope into his pocket. "Am I supposed to pay my round trip train fare out of this three hundred?"

"Of course."

"I thought you'd do better than that for me," Longarm complained. "You know how difficult this assignment will be. I'll probably have to buy a horse, saddle and outfit. That alone will take . . ."

"When you run out of that money wire me for more," Billy snapped as the train jerked and banged into motion.

"What about those two Union Pacific Railroad detectives?"

"They're on board. You'll have to figure out some kind of a way to keep in communication with them. They know that you don't want to be identified as a federal marshal."

Longarm snatched up his canvas duffel bag and started

walking alongside the moving train. "I'll wire you when I light someplace," he called back over his shoulder.

"Wire me the minute you reach Elko!" Billy shouted. "That's where the men you're hunting were last seen."

Longarm grabbed a handrail of the train and threw his duffel on board. The train was gaining speed, but he timed his jump perfectly and leaped onto the platform. Mustering up a smile of good cheer that he didn't feel, Longarm waved back at the fading figure of his boss.

"Billy, don't worry about a thing!" he bellowed, before realizing that his boss wouldn't be able to hear him over the sound of the train's thundering wheels and the screeching of protesting metal being pulled and parted.

Billy waved back at Longarm and then turned and headed back toward downtown. Longarm thought he detected a slump in the man's round shoulders. Maybe Billy hadn't gotten much sleep last night, either. But his lack of sleep would be from worry.

Longarm had never been a worrier. He believed in thinking and expecting things to turn out right. Usually they didn't, but he still thought his attitude was far better than the gloom and doom of so many others he'd met.

"Got your ticket?" the conductor asked.

"No, but I have money to buy one."

"That'll do," the conductor said cheerfully. "Say. Aren't you a federal marshal named Custis Long?"

Longarm gave the man a conspiratorial wink. "Not from this point on for a while."

The conductor was in his early forties. He was momentarily confused by Longarm's reply, but quickly caught on and nodded his head with understanding. "I expect you are going after that bunch of murderers that are robbing Union Pacific trains on the western runs."

"You're a very perceptive man," Longarm told the conductor. "Keep my identity under your cap. All right?"

"Sure thing, but if I recognized you, I'm sure others who work with me will as well. A man of your size and reputation can't easily be ignored."

"That may be the case," Longarm told the conductor, "but there is no sense in spreading my name or identity around."

"Gotcha."

Longarm paid for his ticket, and as he started to enter the coach and take a seat and enjoy a badly needed nap, the conductor touched his sleeve and hissed, "When you catch 'em, you kill them bloody bastards, Marshal!"

Longarm was surprised by the venom.

"You know," the conductor said, trying to force the fury out of his voice. "I work for this line and the men who have been murdered by this gang had all worked for the Union Pacific. We might work for different railroads, but I still consider them as my brothers. And anyone who harms or kills my brothers is my enemy and I want 'em dead."

"I understand," Longarm said, because he really did understand. "I'm a lawman and I feel the same way about my fellow officers. You kill one of us; we're all your sworn enemies."

"Then git 'em!" the conductor hissed. "Shoot 'em to death, beat 'em to death . . . or hang high with a slip instead of a noose so they choke slow and their damned faces turn black with blood. Doesn't matter to us who work for the railroads so long as they die and can't kill anyone anymore."

"I promise you that I'll do my damnedest to bring them to swift justice," Longarm vowed to the man as he moved on into the coach.

• • •

The train was packed as usual and Longarm passed through three passenger cars before he saw Detective Otis Upton and Detective Jason Baxter. Upton barely gave Longarm a glance, but the younger detective stared openly until his partner gave him an elbow to the ribs causing the younger man to grunt.

Longarm passed on to the next coach and finally located an empty seat beside a handsome cattleman who was probably about his own age.

"Seat taken?" Longarm asked.

"Nope," the cattleman answered with a smile. "Sit down and take a load off your feet. My name is Jim Vance."

Longarm saw no point in coming up with some alias that he'd have to try and remember. "Custis Long."

"What's your business?"

"Gambler," Longarm said.

"Well I'll be darned." Vance studied him closely. "You don't *look* like a gambler."

"That's because I don't want to look like one," Longarm explained. "If I wore a fancy suit and tie, diamond stickpin and all that I'd be pegged as a successful gambler and have a hard time getting into an honest game. So I purposefully chose to look like something else."

"You look more like a businessman or a lawman," Jim mused aloud.

"Well, I'm not," Longarm said. "Mind if I smoke a cigar?"

"Hell no."

Longarm drew out one of his cheroots and offered one to Jim who was pleased to accept. They lit up and watched Denver fade into the horizon.

"I'm from Reno," Jim Vance said. "I own a small cattle

ranch called the Circle V located south of Reno in the Washoe Valley. Ever been there?"

"Sure have," Longarm told him. "Washoe Valley is one of the prettiest but windiest places on earth. Windier even than Cheyenne where light horses have to be tied to a post or else they risk being blown away."

Vance laughed. "Well, you got that right. I raise about five hundred head of cattle in that valley and mostly sell them in Carson City and Reno. Some go by train over the Sierras to California for slaughter."

"Sounds like a good thing," Longarm told him.

Vance puffed on the cheroot looking out the window for several minutes, and then asked, "Custis, do you do well at gambling?"

"I do fine," Longarm said. "Try to win more than I lose."

"Maybe we can play a hand or two of poker on this trip."

"I'd rather finish this cigar and take a nap. Had a busy night last night. Kind of feel washed out."

"Wild woman?"

Longarm nodded. "Wild as I'll ever need or want."

Jim smiled. "I come to Denver to visit my brother who has had some bad health problems. I'm a bachelor and I sure do appreciate Denver women. My brother, he thinks I come just to see him, but it's also because I know a few of your ladies."

"You ever marry?" Longarm asked.

"Nope. Never will. Can't stand the idea of a noose around my neck . . . not to mention a ribbon around my pole." Jim winked. "Know what I mean?"

"Sure do. I never married either. A gambler is a poor prospect for matrimony."

Vance produced a silver flask. He uncorked it and said, "Well, here's to us bachelors. May we live fast, but die easy and smiling."

"Amen," Longarm said, declining a drink as the rolling grassland of northern Colorado rolled by.

He did take a nap and Jim woke him up as they neared Cheyenne. The tall, Nevada cattleman shook Longarm's hand and said, "I expect I'll be seeing you on the Union Pacific. How far are you going?"

"Elko."

Jim's eyebrows arched in question. "Why Elko? I wouldn't think that that would be much of a place to gamble."

"You'd be surprised," Longarm said. "There's a lot of money in that railroad and cattle town. And best of all it isn't overrun with gamblers."

"Ahh," the cattleman said, "I get your drift. You got this gambling thing all figured out, I reckon."

"Close enough to keep myself in high clover most of the time. But, like all gambling men, I have my losing streaks when Lady Luck seems to take a long holiday."

"Know what you mean, partner. The cattle business has almost as many lean years as fat ones. I try my best to set aside a nest egg when beef prices are high so that I can survive the tough times."

"Did you start out as a cowboy?"

"Sure did! My father drove cattle up the old Chisholm Trail. I missed that, but I was forking broncs when I was still in diapers."

Longarm smiled. "There are a lot of mustangs in Nevada. Do you hunt them?"

"Not unless I have to," Vance assured him. "See you later."

Longarm nodded. Jim Vance seemed like a right fine fellow. Longarm noticed that the man wore expensive boots and carried a very fine Colt sidearm that rested in a tooled leather holster supported by an equally handsome gun belt. No doubt about it that the Nevada rancher was at least semi-prosperous and that he liked the ladies and he liked to gamble. That could be a problem later because Longarm really wasn't that good of a gambler.

Well, he could worry about that later, if it became an issue.

When the train pulled into Cheyenne, Longarm prepared to disembark like everyone else. You couldn't stay on the Denver Pacific because it went to a roundhouse and then headed back south to Denver.

He saw the railroad detectives standing on the platform out of the rain. Young Baxter started toward him and when he was close, dropped a small piece of paper before moving on. Longarm picked it up and read, *Otis wants you to stay here and take the next train after we leave.*

Longarm glanced over at Otis Upton. The man was trying not to appear as if he were watching Longarm, but he obviously was waiting for an answer to his written note.

Longarm decided to turn his back on the man and ignore him. Braving the rain he started to leave for a drink at the saloon while he waited for the westbound to take him to Nevada, but Detective Upton came up to him in a hurry.

"Gawdamn you!" the man hissed. "We can't all go on the same train! You wait here and take the next one."

"Go screw yourself," Longarm said pleasantly. "I'm leaving Cheyenne on the next train and you can do the same or not . . . it makes no difference to me."

"We'll see about that!"

Longarm didn't know what that was supposed to mean

and he really didn't care. The railroad detectives weren't in his plans and he doubted very much that he was in theirs.

So be it. They would all be on their own just the way he'd expected from the moment he'd met the two detectives in Denver. And to hell with co-operation. Cooperation with incompetents like those two could get a good lawman killed quicker than he could blink.

Longarm was a man who liked to work alone and this manhunt was going to be every man for himself. He tugged the brim of his Stetson down over his face to sheet off the rain and slogged through the mud into the middle of Cheyenne.

Chapter 5

It was a three hour layover before he could catch the west-bound Union Pacific so Longarm made a few stops mainly just to kill time. First he had a meal at the Roundup Café where he knew the owner and the help. After exchanging pleasantries and listening to them gripe for an entire hour about the endless rain they were getting this spring Longarm trudged over to a gun shop and bought some extra ammunition for his double action Colt .44-.40 which he wore over his left hip, butt forward. He did not consider himself a shootist or fast draw artist, but Longarm knew that he was quicker than ninety percent of the men he'd ever have to brace. And, when he did expect to come up against a faster draw, he always shot first and asked questions later . . . if his opponent was still breathing.

"How's it going, Art?" he asked the man who owned the gun shop.

Art Haskins was an ex-lawman in his forties. He'd been a town marshal and then a Texas Ranger. Longarm knew and liked Art although the man was prone to look at the dark side of life.

Art glanced up and gave Longarm his best attempt at a grin. "Business is slower'n molasses," he said with a weary sigh of resignation. "I haven't sold one dang thing this entire day. Only sold one pistol all week and that was to an Indian that didn't have but three dollars. Sold him an old Army cap and ball revolver. I told the Indian that it didn't shoot straight and might even blow up in his face, but he didn't care."

"Well," Longarm said, looking down at the newspaper that Art had been poring over, "at least you're getting the extra time to catch up on your reading."

"Not sure that I should," Art grumped. "Why, I've been reading about how Congress just passed a bill restricting the immigration of Chinese. Then, President Hayes said he'd veto the bill."

"What's wrong with Chinese?" Longarm asked with idle curiosity. "If it wasn't for them, the Union Pacific would never have been able to get track laid down over the Sierras."

"The problem," Art explained, "is that Californians say there are too damned many Chinese. The people and politicians of that state claim that there are almost three hundred thousand of 'em, mostly livin' in San Francisco. I guess there's a lot of white folks that feel the Chinaman is takin' away too many jobs."

"They work cheap," Longarm admitted. "But they're generally sober and hardworking people. I guess that after they built this railroad everyone expected them to go back home to China, but a lot didn't. Things are probably tough taters in China, but I don't know 'cause I've never been overseas."

"Yeah," Art said, folding up his newspaper. "I hear that things are really tough in China. All they got to eat is rice and noodles . . . maybe a skinny chicken once a year or so. No wonder the celestials are so underfed. You ever seen a fat Chinaman, Custis?"

Longarm thought about it. "Don't believe I ever did."

"Well, that just goes to prove the point," Art said, folding his arms across his chest as if that permanently settled the matter.

Longarm wasn't sure what point it proved, but he nodded in agreement. "Everything else in that newspaper okay?"

"Depends on your point of view. For example, it says that the first public electrical system in this country was just installed in Cleveland, Ohio. Shoot, I'll bet it'll be about a hundred years before Cheyenne ever gets public electricity installed. Long after my bones are all picked clean by maggots while I take the long dirt nap."

"Yeah, probably," Longarm said, deciding he'd heard enough of the latest news from Art. "I could use a box of cartridges. Maybe I'll also have a look at your rifles for sale."

Art perked up a bit at the prospect of selling a rifle. "What kind are you interested in?"

"Winchester repeater. Nothing fancy. I'm kinda short of cash. Don't mind if it's a little banged up so long as it shoots straight and won't jam up in a gunfight."

"Got just the one for you!" Art turned around and removed a Winchester from the rifle rack. Its stock was scarred and chipped and it looked as if it had had a lot of hard use, but when Longarm hefted the rifle and then worked the lever action, it was slick and quick.

"As you are aware, I test fire everything I sell," Art said. "And I wouldn't sell a bad rifle to any man, let alone a lawman of your reputation."

"How much?"

"For you, only twenty dollars."

The price was good so Longarm didn't haggle. He paid for the rifle and bought a little more ammunition just to be on the safe side. Art's used firearms were cheaper than he could buy them for in Denver, but he was a bit high on the price of his ammunition.

"Better load it right now," Art said. "Nothing more useless than an empty weapon."

Longarm nodded in agreement. "How's the town doin' these days?"

"Same as always. We're in the middle of spring roundup so most of the cowboys are out on the range even in this foul weather. Sure will be glad when the sun shines again."

"Yeah," Longarm agreed, "but remember that all this rain will really green up this country and make for a good year for cattlemen."

"I know. I know. And with money in everyone's pocket some will trickle down to me . . . I hope. But it's slim pickin's in this business. A fella name Bafford just opened a gun shop over on the next block."

Haskins rolled his eyes. "Can you imagine? I can't hardly make a living here and this joker opens up a shop just like mine. I ought to go over and tell the fool what he's up against in this two-bit train town, but he probably wouldn't pay me no mind. The fool would just think I was trying to scare him off so I could fatten my own calf."

"Probably," Longarm said. "Is Marshal Pat McPeak in today?"

"Hell if I know. Probably is. He doesn't like to go out in the bad weather. Stays there in his office like an old rooster on his roost. If we had any real trouble, he'd probably send for me to form a posse. He's lazier than a fat lizard. Kinda looks like one too."

"I guess I'll go by and say hello to him."

Haskins lowered his voice even though they were all alone in his little shop. "You're out here this time because of that murdering train gang, ain't ya?"

Longarm dipped his chin.

"Good luck with that bunch. Hope you're not alone on this job. Them boys are *real* killers."

"So I hear."

"You ain't workin' alone, are you?"

Longarm didn't want to tip his hand to anyone. Art was a good man, but he had a loose tongue. He liked to spin stories about his old days when he was a town tamer and Texas Ranger. But Longarm didn't have that much time to listen so he said goodbye and went over to see Marshal McPeak who just might have some new information on the train gang.

"Howdy, Marshal," Longarm said, coming in the door and catching the man dozing at his desk.

The lawman looked happy to see Custis. "Well, if it ain't United States Deputy Marshal Long! As I live and breathe, how are you, Custis?"

"I'm fine," he said.

"You been beatin' up on old ladies again?" the marshal asked with a grin and a good natured wink. "Those knuckles of yours are sure raw lookin' today."

"No old ladies," Longarm replied with a straight face. "Just lots of old, weak men."

Marshal McPeak laughed as if that was the funniest thing he'd heard in years. When he finally stopped his guffawing he crawled out of his office chair and stuck out his

49

big hand. McPeak wasn't tall, but he was stout and even though he was in his fifties, still a powerful man. Longarm knew that Art was correct about Pat McPeak being a tad lazy, but the man was brave and he knew this was why the city fathers of Cheyenne had no intentions of replacing him with a younger marshal.

"Coffee?" McPeak asked, gesturing toward a pot.

"Sure."

Longarm and the town marshal sat for a while swapping lies and then Longarm got down to the more serious subject of the train robberies and murders. "Pat," he said, "I was hoping you might be able to give me some inside information about what we're up against with this train robbery gang."

McPeak leaned back in his chair, laced is fingers over his belly and frowned. "Tell me what you already know so I won't waste our time."

"I don't know too much," Longarm said, telling the man what he'd been told by his boss before leaving Denver.

"Well, you know damned near as much as I do," McPeak said. "But there is a small thing or two that you didn't mention."

"What's that?"

"Those train robbers always have a couple of their boys hiding out with escape horses. And I'm told they are *fast* horses. Top quality and twice what they need so the robbers can relay 'em for at least a hundred miles in any direction."

Longarm frowned. "That would mean they should be able to outrun any pursuit by lawmen."

"Exactly," McPeak said. "And, if I were looking for that bunch, I'd be keeping a pretty close eye on who is buying the finest horses to be found out in the West. I know for a fact that they aren't mustangs. I also have heard from passengers who have seen the gang ride away that their mounts are tall, like racehorses. Maybe even Kentucky thoroughbreds or at least crossbreds."

"I hadn't heard that before," Longarm said.

"No, I didn't think you had," McPeak replied. "But those kinds of horses, in those kinds of numbers, would stand out. Stand out more than the men who rode 'em. So I'd look for a bunch of tall, fast racehorses. You find them; you'll probably find a link to that gang."

Longarm was glad that he had stopped by the town marshal's office. "Anything else?"

"You've heard that one of the gang is a giant?"

"Yes I have. Also that another is pretty small. Not a midget, but close."

"They'd stand out together, that's for certain," McPeak said. "And I heard that in this latest heist, they have a marksman or two in their midst."

"What do you mean?"

"I mean," McPeak said, "that when they robbed that train outa Elko, the railroad had a couple of hired riflemen hidden in a boxcar. The idea was that they'd open up on the gang and try to kill as many as they could before they galloped away."

Longarm waited. "And?"

"The railroad's hidden riflemen were no match for the robbers. They winged one of 'em but then two of the robbers jumped off their horses with big scoped rifles and shot the pair of railroad men to death."

"That a fact?" This wasn't good news to Longarm. Not good news at all.

"It is a fact. And I'm surprised that the railroad hasn't told you about that. Maybe they didn't tell you because they didn't want to scare you off."

"What you're telling me about the fast horses and the scoped rifles does make things a damned sight more dangerous."

"Of course! How you gonna take 'em on, Custis? Not by yourself, I sure hope."

Longarm shook his head. "To tell you the truth, Pat, I just haven't put a lot of thought into it yet. I only heard about the gang yesterday and I don't expect to be in their territory for another few days. By then, I expect to hatch a plan of some sort."

"Well," McPeak said, "I don't envy you and I hope you got help. Do you know the town marshal in Elko?"

"Bruce Atherton?"

"He quit. New Marshal is named Wyatt Dowd."

"Never heard of him."

"Neither have I," McPeak said. "He's probably a greenhorn that the town council over there got for beans and a bed. I doubt he'll be of much help, but it don't hurt to ask."

Longarm nodded in agreement. "Do you know anything about two railroad detectives named Otis Upton and Jason Baxter?"

"Sure, I know of 'em."

"What did you think?"

"I liked the younger man, Baxter. He seemed like he had a good head on his shoulders. No braggart, like so many of the young ones these days. As for Otis Upton, I wouldn't trust him any further than I could throw the man."

"You think he's just all talk?"

"I just think he's out to feather his own nest. Detective Upton desperately wants to be the one that puts the coffin lid down on that bunch and he wants to become famous. I believe that a man like that is dangerous, not only to himself, but to those around him. What I'm tellin' you, Custis, is don't tell him what you don't have to tell him. Get my drift?"

"Yeah. That was my own impression of Detective Upton. I am sort of counting on young Detective Baxter to help, if I get in a bad fix."

"He's pretty young, but I think he's a gamer," McPeak said. "Strikes me as the kind of a man who wouldn't run off and leave you in a bad fix."

"And Upton would?"

"Maybe." McPeak wagged his double chins. "Just maybe he would, if he didn't think he could get famous by helping a fellow lawman."

Longarm thanked Marshal Pat McPeak, especially for his information on the racehorses and the scoped rifles. When he left the man's office, he was feeling a bit out of sorts. Hell, he didn't have the money to buy a fast horse to go after the gang and he didn't even have a high-powered scoped rifle.

Not to mention the fact that he was far outnumbered.

Longarm was going to head for the Palace Saloon when he saw the railroad detectives huddled under a porch trying to look as if they were talking to each other and having a good time.

Instead, they looked ridiculous.

There was no one out on the sidewalks in this rain so Longarm thought to hell with it and just walked up to the two detectives. "Waitin' for me?" he asked, knowing that they were.

"We shouldn't be seen together!" Upton hissed.

Longarm turned full circle and confronted the older man. "Ain't anybody watching us. Nobody is outside in this downpour except us fools. What do you want?"

"What did you learn from Marshal McPeak?" Upton demanded. "He wouldn't tell us jackshit."

"I didn't learn jackshit from the man. He doesn't know anything that you don't know already." That wasn't true, but it was all right as far as Longarm was concerned. He needed an edge on the information and besides these two would learn about the fast horses and scoped rifles as soon as they got to Elko. So what difference did his silence make now?

"I think he musta told you something important," Upton persisted. "You wouldn't hold back from us, would you?"

"Hell no," Longarm said, trying to look offended. "We're all working together, isn't that right?"

"That's right," Upton said.

"That's right," Baxter echoed.

"Good. It's cold and miserable out here. Why don't you boys buy me a drink at the Palace Saloon."

"Are you crazy!" Upton snapped. "We're not supposed to know each other."

"Well," Longarm said, "in that case, see you later, maybe."

He left the two Union Pacific detectives in the rain and headed for the saloon. There was a woman who tended bar there named Daisy. He couldn't remember her last name and perhaps that was because she had never told it to him. All he remembered was that Daisy had had a weakness for him.

Longarm pulled out his Ingersol railroad watch and consulted it for the time. He had about an hour and a half before the train left the station. That, he thought with a sly smile, was far more time than he needed to get cozy with Daisy and well reacquainted.

Just thinking about the woman and a whiskey made Longarm walk faster.

54

Chapter 6

"Well as I live and breathe if it isn't the famous Marshal Custis Long!" Daisy cried, hurrying across the saloon floor and throwing her arms around him a moment before delivering a long, wet kiss. "How are you, darling?"

"I'm doing just fine," he said, feeling better in her arms than he had all day. "But I sure could use something to warm up my belly given this foul weather."

"I'll bring you a glass of our best whiskey, Custis."

Daisy was tall and statuesque with glossy black hair and high cheekbones. Once she had told him she was a quarter Cheyenne and Longarm had no reason to doubt that. Daisy wasn't a prostitute. She poured drinks and served them to customers. And once in a while, if she really liked a man, she went upstairs to be with him and told him afterward that he could pay her an amount equal to the pleasure she had given. However, if the man was broke and Daisy liked him very much, he got it for free and without hard feelings.

It was a unique way of doing things, but Longarm was

quite sure that Daisy made far more money from her special customers than any prostitute in Cheyenne. Also, because she was very choosy about her men, they all treated her like a queen.

"Here you are, Custis. This one is on me."

Longarm raised his glass to the tall, striking woman. "Daisy my dear, you look as if life here is treating you very well."

"I get by just fine," she said. "Actually, I took the train to California for two months this past winter and laid in the warm sun. I walked on the sandy beaches near old Monterey. I watched migrating gray whales just off the coast and I'll never forget how big and beautiful they were and how small they made me feel. And I got a good tan, not that I needed one with my skin."

That was true. Daisy not only had the high cheekbones of a Cheyenne, she had their coloring. The only strange thing was that her eyes were blue and her nose was sharp rather than broad. Maybe some of her European ancestors were from Scandinavia.

"So what brings you out in this weather?" Daisy asked. "As if I couldn't guess."

Longarm nodded to the bartender, and wishing some privacy, he said to the woman, "Why don't we go over to a table where we can talk in private? I haven't got much time, Daisy. I'm catching the westbound out today."

"Doesn't leave for a while yet," she assured him as she kissed his lips again. "So why don't we go upstairs to my room and talk?"

"I'd like that just fine."

Daisy led the way up the stairs to the second floor room where she lived and occasionally pleasured her small group of very favored customers. Longarm placed his coat and hat on a rack and looked around the nicely decorated room. "Not a thing has changed."

"It hardly ever does in Cheyenne. What happened to your hands and your neck?" She made a face. "That thing on your neck looks like ringworm or something equally awful."

"It's a cigar burn," he explained. "I got into a bit of a scrap before leaving Denver. Nothing much."

"And you've lost a little weight," she said, coming over and wrapping her arms around his waist and giving him another deep kiss. "I think I'll have to write a letter to your boss and tell him that you and me ought to take a long, romantic vacation. Maybe even go to New York or New Orleans. How'd you like that, Custis?"

"Sounds great," he said trying to sound enthusiastic. "But I'm afraid my boss wouldn't let me go right now. I've got some very important business to handle in Nevada."

"Don't tell me that they sent you out to stop that gang of train robbers and murderers that just hit the train outside of Elko!"

"Yep."

Her face clouded. "Oh, Custis, you're going to get into something really bad with that bunch. How many men are working with you?"

"Two railroad detectives," he said, not wanting to elaborate. "But I can call in the cavalry if I get in a real tough situation."

Daisy took his glass and went over to the window where she tossed its contents out in the back alley. Longarm frowned in puzzlement. "Why'd you do that?"

"I've got better hooch for you up here," she replied, filling them both glasses of expensive bourbon and then raising her glass in a toast. "To us someday on vacation together where it is fun, and warm and it won't rain."

Longarm raised his own glass to the toast and studied Daisy closely. "You're looking even prettier than I'd remembered. You ought to go to California more often."

"I plan to. I might retire there, Custis. Interested?"

"In retiring in California?"

"That's right. Specifically in Monterey which I fell in love with at first sight."

He shook his head. "Not at all my style."

She looked genuinely disappointed. "You've probably never even been there."

"That's right," he told her. "But I've heard that it's damp and foggy. Daisy, I like clear, fresh air."

She laughed. "How about Lake Tahoe, then?"

"Sorry, but that's too cold in the winter."

Daisy set her glass down and kissed Longarm again. "You are a very hard man to tempt."

"Depends on the temptation," he said, draining his own glass and taking the woman in his arms. "I do have one major weakness."

"Is that right?" she asked in mock curiosity as she looked up at his face with a smile of anticipation. "And what is that?"

"*You*," he said, feeling the heat rise in his loins.

"Well, Marshal Custis Long, in that case, don't you think we ought to satisfy that weakness before it gets the best of you?" she asked as her hands slid down his lean, muscular frame.

"I definitely think we should," he assured her.

Longarm quickly removed her clothes and then he licked her nipples until they were as hard as chocolate drops. Falling onto the bed in a tumble of laughter and passion, he plunged into her honey pot driving his thick shaft to the hilt.

"Oh, my, you feel right at home," she moaned, hugging him tightly and then wrapping her long, silky legs around his waist. "I missed you, Custis. Please don't rush me too much. Forget the damned train for a while."

"I will," he promised.

"You know I'd just like to lie here very still and feel you deep inside me for a few minutes."

"We can do that," he said, kissing her lips then her cheeks and finally her long, lustrous black hair.

"Why don't you just quit your job and we'll go on vacation tomorrow?" she said dreamily.

"I can't," he replied beginning to stir her gently. "You know that my job is important to me."

"Yes," she said, her eyes getting misty. "I do. But one day you're going to end up on the undertaker's cold slab. It's just a matter of how long you can defy the odds."

"Shhh," he whispered. "Let's not talk like that today. Some other time, maybe. But not now."

"You're right," she said, squeezing him with all the strength in her limbs. "Let's just lose ourselves in each other and see if it can feel like a lifetime."

Longarm began to make love to this beautiful woman using every bit of his skill and experience. He knew from past times exactly how Daisy liked it and he meant to satisfy her first. So he continued his slow, even strokes for almost a half hour until even his toes began to tingle. By then Daisy was thrashing underneath him, and when she bit his shoulder and her body convulsed in a shuddering climax, Longarm knew it was his own time.

He began to move into and out of her faster and harder until he groaned and filled her with torrents of his seed. Then he kissed away the sweet perspiration on her upper lip and rolled aside.

"Custis," she whispered, "you know I take a few men out of choice . . . but you are and have always been my most special."

"I'll bet you say that to all of them," he teased.

"No," she told him, her face close and serious. "I don't."

He heard the train's whistle and jumped off the bed.

"Don't be alarmed," she told him. "They blow it a half hour before departure then again at fifteen minutes."

"That's right," he said, "I'd forgotten."

"But you won't forget me and our vacation?"

"Not a chance," he said, dressing.

"You be careful and stop by on your way back through Cheyenne for a longer visit."

"I will."

Daisy got up and poured them both another shot of bourbon. "To our promised vacation where it is dry and sunny," she said raising her glass.

"To our promised vacation." Longarm meant it, too. And nothing would stop him from sometime going on a vacation with Daisy except maybe a bullet from a high-powered and telescoped rifle.

But he didn't need to tell Daisy that so he just smiled, buckled on his gunbelt and kissed her goodbye.

Chapter 7

With only minutes to spare Longarm boarded the train rolling west out of Cheyenne and bought another ticket. He wasn't familiar with this conductor and that was surprising since he rode the Union Pacific so frequently. A lot of the federal marshals in the Denver office wanted to stick close to home, but Longarm much preferred long-distance rail travels. One advantage of working out in big country was that his federal authority tether was stretched far thinner so that he enjoyed more autonomy. Another thing was that Longarm had been traveling so many years that he had many distant good friends and acquaintances like Daisy that gave spice to his life. And finally, Longarm genuinely liked to see new country. To his way of thinking, Colorado was about as pretty a place as man could ever expect to find. But he'd also cultivated a love for the wide open prairies of Wyoming, the beauty of the Sonoran Desert down in Arizona and the towering Sierra Nevada Mountains which, in their own way, were every bit as stunning as the Rockies. Oh, and maybe his favorite was the Grand

Canyon and the Painted Desert. He even had hunted up an exceptional piece of petrified wood that he kept as a lucky talisman.

The first part of his railroad journey was through the spectacular Laramie Mountains and it was always one of Longarm's favorite stretches. At this time of year the rugged Laramie peaks were still capped with deep snow. Longarm stood out on the open platform between two passenger coaches and smoked his cheroots enjoying the magnificent scenery.

After struggling over the mountains and down into the little town of Laramie the country flattened out in western Wyoming but there were still plenty of antelope, wild mustangs and cattle scattered across the grassy hills and valleys to watch. He saw cowboys on the spring roundup and most of them waved at him in a friendly greeting.

It wasn't until his train entered Utah and passed Promontory Point where the great Transcontinental Railroad Race had ended in 1869 that the land turned hard, desolate and dry. But Longarm didn't even mind that because he just liked to see all the different landscapes of the vast western frontier unfold. This was Mormon country were it was often very difficult to eke out a living. But many Mormons obvious succeeded here providing they had good water and enough land to run their sheep, cattle and to irrigate their farmland.

Sometimes, Longarm would also see isolated bands of Paiutes, but never more than a dozen grouped together. He would wave but they rarely waved in return. The Paiute were a tough, nomadic breed of Indians that wanted nothing to do with the white man and had once even staged a rebellion that had temporarily shut down the fabled Pony Express.

Now, the Paiute seemed to have decided to go their own way and that meant sticking to the driest and most inhospitable sections of the Great Basin where there was nothing buried or growing on their land that could profit or attract white men.

Longarm had kept mostly to himself on this train trip. He listened for gossip about the train robbery gang and heard all sorts of wild stories. A wealthy Englishman touring America with his bride swore that the train thieves and murderers were actually Chiricahua Apache Indians disguised as white men and led by the famous Indian Chief Cochise. The Englishman had this preposterous theory that Blackfoot Indians had entered a deal with Cochise who was now plundering the trains. According the Englishmen, the bounty taken from the train robberies was split between the two tribes and then secreted off to Canada by the Blackfoot and to Mexico by Cochise and his Apache warriors.

This ridiculous idea gained more and more credence as the Union Pacific chugged westward among ignorant easterners who didn't even realize that Cochise had died in 1874 and had been given a secret burial somewhere in Southern Arizona's wild and nearly inaccessible Dragoon Mountains.

The wild and excited speculation about Cochise and the Apache being behind the train robberies made Longarm laugh out loud.

One afternoon, he was standing on the open platform between the coaches in one of the most desolate parts of the eastern Nevada high desert when he heard the passenger coach door open behind him. The door's rusty hinges needed oiling and their protest was an assault on the eardrums.

"Marshal Long, now that we're finally approaching Elko, it's time that we had a private little conversation,"

Detective Otis Upton announced. "One that I feel is very much overdue."

"Good," Longarm said, turning to face the railroad detective. "We never even settled on a code that we could use to communicate."

Upton pursed his lips for a moment in feigned concentration. "How about *'Intruder'*?"

"That's an odd code name. I take it that you are referring to me."

"Exactly," Detective Upton said.

"Well, I don't really like that code name," Longarm told the sarcastic railroad detective. "I'm afraid you'll have to think of another."

"What have you learned so far about the gang?" Upton asked, suddenly changing the subject.

"Nothing much. I'm enjoying all the wild and nonsensical speculation by the Englishman that Cochise and his band of Apaches are behind these train attacks."

"Yes, that is completely ridiculous, but it does seem to have gained the favor of many of our eastern and European passengers," Upton said. "Have you heard anything about the gang having telescopic rifles or racehorses?"

"I have heard those rumors," Longarm admitted, not wanting to say more.

"They are *not* rumors," Upton assured him. "They're eyewitness facts."

"Then we'll just have to deal with that somehow," Longarm said, turning to gaze out toward the endless ocean of sagebrush, rocks and pinion pines. He saw an immense dust devil dancing off to the north, one large enough to tear big pieces of sagebrush out of the earth and swirl them upward in a towering funnel.

But Upton was focused on Longarm. "Besides the code, I wanted to ask you to stay in Elko when we arrive there."

Longarm tore his attention from the dust devil and regarded Upton with unconcealed skepticism. "Oh? And why should I do that?"

"We'll need someone in Elko at all times to help supply myself and Detective Baxter out in the field. And also to hold their ear to the ground . . . so to speak . . . keeping good communications flowing between ourselves and our superiors."

Longarm shook his head with disbelief and turned back to the railroad detective. "Upton, I'll be damned if I've come all the way out here to Nevada in order to be stuck in Elko as a messenger and supply boy for you and your junior grade lawman."

"Then you intend to go out into the field no matter what I say?"

"It's not the field, it's the *sagebrush*," Longarm corrected. "And yes, I'll hunt this gang wherever they go and I won't stop until I've caught or killed them."

"Or they've killed you."

"That is possible," Longarm conceded. "But the possibility of getting my ticket permanently punched is always part of my job. When I pinned on my officer's badge, that's the responsibility I freely accepted."

"I can understand that," Upton told him. "I'm a little older than you and I know the meaning of danger and risk. I've been in a lot of bad fights and always managed to . . . if not win . . . then at least survive."

Longarm believed the man, but thought Upton was bragging a bit to even mention the fact. "Good for you, Detective."

Upton squinted out into the passing desert, his eyes reaching out into the distance as he carefully formed his next words. "Marshal Long, I'm sure you don't give a damn, but when I was quite young . . . only a little boy . . . I dreamed of being an American hero. And when I enlisted in the Union Army, I thought my time had finally come to be that hero I had wanted to be since childhood. At the start of the war I was commissioned a captain and I was soon leading a patrol of brave cavalrymen on dangerous raids behind the Confederate lines. Our lives were always in great danger, but I kept my men alive and I was starting to gain a reputation that would equal that of George Custer for boldness and daring. But then I was deceived by one of my own men and led into a deadly trap near Charleston."

Upton took a deep, shuddering breath and expelled it slowly. His expression had turned gray, as bleak and impenetrable as coastal fog. "Out of twenty-three cavalrymen I commanded that terrible day only myself and two others survived . . . one being the traitor whom I promptly shot."

Longarm's interest was piqued. "So what happened to the only other survivor besides yourself to survive that raid?"

"He was decorated for bravery. But because I had been deceived by one of my own men, leading to the death of almost every man under my command, I was busted to private. Six months later, the war ended." Upton took a ragged breath. "I didn't even get a pension, much less a letter of commendation for all the successful raids I'd conducted and the rebels that I'd helped kill in the gallant line of duty."

Longarm had listened respectfully, but now he had heard enough to understand what made this man tick. "So you were betrayed and lost your chance of being a hero during the War Between the States. And then you went to work as a local lawman."

"That's my story."

Longarm said, "And I'd bet my last dollar that local law enforcement didn't work out very well for you either. Once more you were not fully appreciated or rewarded. Am I correct, Detective Upton?"

Upton's cheeks darkened with anger when he realized Longarm was not at all sympathetic. "People never appreciated the risks I took and gave me my just due! I *tamed* towns, Marshal Long. I have stood in the middle of a dirty main street and faced gunfighters! And I killed them, by gawd! I never ran nor was I ever beaten or humiliated."

"Congratulations," Longarm replied, "it's a shame that you never received the glory you have always desired. But few of us do. What's important now, however, is that you seem to believe that capturing the train robbers is your last chance to grab the golden ring."

"That's crudely put, but true. I'm older than you and I'm fast running out of time."

"Upton, I know you won't do it, but you should retire *today*," Longarm told the railroad detective with unusual bluntness. "Do it when we reach Elko and save yourself a lot of misery and possibly even your life."

"I can't quit! I have very little savings and I have not yet fulfilled my destiny."

Longarm had heard enough. This man was driven by delusions of grandeur and consumed by demons formed from his earliest years. Longarm tossed his unfinished cigar out onto the railroad bed. He started to excuse himself and return to his seat when Upton suddenly drew his pistol and shoved it into Longarm's belly.

"What are you doing?"

Upton cocked back the hammer of his pistol. They were alone on the platform and the clanging of steel and banging of railroad car couplings would drown out a pistol shot.

"You wouldn't listen, would you," Upton said, his face turning into a dark mask twisting with hatred. "You wouldn't let an older man fulfill his destiny because you want all the glory for yourself. Isn't that right, Marshal Custis Long?"

"No!"

Although it was not warm even in the high desert at this time of year and the wind was whistling in his ears, Long-arm could begin to feel sweat trickle out of his armpits. Otis Upton had a look of madness in his eyes. . . . madness and desperation. Longarm knew he was about to die if he did not use all of his wits and get lucky. "Look, Upton," he began, "maybe you were right and I should stay in Elko to coordinate things. And you can call me 'Intruder' or even asshole. I don't care. But let's try to be *reasonable* lawmen and work together to stop this gang. Upton, put the gun away and we'll sort our differences out."

The man shook his head. "Not possible. I know that you're just saying that to save your own life, but it's too late now and it would never work. You're basically a loner and so am I. Two lone wolfs on a manhunt and one of us has to die."

Longarm found that his mouth was suddenly so dry that he could barely speak. But he *had* to speak so he said, "You've been under a lot of strain, Detective. You're not thinking clearly right now. I've got some money that will help you get a new start in a new part of the country. There's over two hundred dollars in my wallet right now. It'll hold you until you find a job that isn't so tough. You don't have to . . ."

"Shut up and turn around."

Longarm knew that he had no choice but to do as this man demanded. And yet . . . if he did turn around, he would get a bullet in the back and that would be the end. His body would be thrown off the side of the train in this empty wilderness and maybe never found until it was just a jumble of broken bones picked clean by the coyotes and the birds and finally insects.

"Upton," he said, trying desperately to think of some words that would save his life. "You'll be caught if you kill me and you'll hang."

"How so?" the man said, eyebrows raised in question. "No one will hear the shot and I'll just go on back to my seat as if I'd returned from a breath of fresh air. And even if your body is found . . . and I sure as hell won't report it missing . . . then so what as far as I'm concerned?"

"They will know my death was no accident because my body would be found with a bullet in it."

"Yes," Upton agreed, his eyes burning with a strange and intensive light. "So someone will say you probably shot yourself. Lawmen do that sometimes, you know."

"Dammit, that won't wash!"

"Then they'll say you were robbed," Upton countered, seeming now to almost enjoy himself. "Oh, I almost forgot about the robbery motive. I'll have your wallet and that money now. Reach for it with your left hand and if you make one false move, I'll blow your guts all over the roadbed."

Longarm slowly reached into his coat and gave up his wallet. His armpits were leaking faster.

"Look" he said, "I . . ."

"The talking is over, Marshal. And I have noticed that fine gold watch chain on your vest. Let me have it, please."

Longarm finally saw a light at the end of a dark tunnel

leading to his grave. His watch chain had a railroad watch attached to one end, but a small hide out derringer attached to the other. If he could just get it free he might be able to kill Upton an instant before the man pulled the trigger of his Colt revolver.

"As you wish," Longarm said. "But I still have a few things that I need for you to hear."

"I'll listen to your last foolish words." Upton shifted on the balls of his feet then leaned up against the short iron guard rail that sided the little platform. "But while you're talking, slowly hand over that gold pocket watch."

Longarm wanted to keep the man's attention so he just said the first things that came to his mind as his hand eased the derringer from his vest pocket. The derringer was solid brass, a deadly little twin-barrel weapon that had never failed to catch an enemy by surprise and put him six feet underground.

"I was going to say that you really need to put your gun away and rethink this whole situation," Longarm said, giving the detective one last chance to turn back.

Upton almost laughed. "Is that it? That's all you have to say as your final words? Don't you want to beg for your life?"

"I've never begged and I sure as hell won't start now."

Upton shrugged. "Then in that case . . ."

"Look at my hand, Upton."

Upton's eyes dropped to what he thought would be a fine gold watch and chair. Instead, he saw the derringer in Longarm's hand and pulled the trigger of his Colt without an instant of hesitation.

Longarm had fired at almost the exact same split second. The sound of their weapons was somewhat muffled by the closeness of their bodies and the hammering train, but it was loud and Longarm instantly knew that he was hit hard by a bullet.

However, in less time than it took a man to blink, he saw Upton's eyes dilate with shock and Longarm was sure that he had drilled the railroad detective dead center. Longarm gave him a second dose of lead from the other barrel of the derringer. Unable to keep from falling off the train he grabbed Upton by the front of his coat and dragged him overboard.

Together they plummeted off the train to strike the side of the railroad bed. Longarm's head slammed into loose cinders and his body went cartwheeling end over end into darkness.

Chapter 8

It was dark when he finally awoke. Longarm could hear a pack of coyotes howling somewhere nearby in the brush. He had left the rain back around Salt Lake City. Out here in the middle of the Great Basin the clear night sky looked like a great fire-blackened bowl peppered with buckshot. The moon was a wedge of lemon and the air was cold enough so that he could send his breath clouds toward the silent heavens.

Longarm didn't move for several minutes, just admiring the sky and trying to stop the slow spinning of his vision. When the stars and constellations at last froze themselves he reached down and touched the source of his pain.

He felt the bullet wound, the surrounding caked blood and the still leaking trickle of blood flow. *I've been shot in the side,* he thought. *Pretty bad, too.*

Longarm dragged his handkerchief from his pocket and with all of his will tried to shove it into the wound.

He fainted.

Much later when he awoke the stars had moved around

in the sky and there was just the faintest hint of a sunrise to the east. Daylight was coming in the next hour and Longarm was content to lie still, breathe deep and wait for the dawn and fresh hope.

But it was cold, so very cold.

He waited and watched the sunrise strengthen across the sky and the low, rocky hills. He admired how the ridges and mountains turned crimson along their crests as the golden glow of morning slowly pushed the night shadows aside and let the earth take on dimension. Details that he had only seen in silhouette moments earlier now took form, shape and color.

Longarm craned his head around this way and that until his focus rested on the rails going off into the east and the west seeming to merge into infinity.

"I'm in a bad place here," he told himself. "I'm fifty miles at least from Elko and even farther from any other known settlement."

A wren flitted through the brush and an owl hooted to signal the end of its nocturnal hunting.

Longarm studied the rails for several minutes. Those nearest him were a good ten feet higher than his head and rested on the hump of the railroad bed. Not far away was a low train trestle under which there was a streambed filled with the barest trickle of spring runoff from the Ruby Mountains or some closer mountain range.

"Water," he said out loud as he stared at the tiny flow and suddenly felt very thirsty.

The single word and the sight of the small stream that now glistened in the glow of early morning gave him an immediate need and purpose. And purpose would give him strength and strength would give him the will to find a way to survive.

Longarm twisted around to look behind him and saw Detective Otis Upton's crumpled body. The man had apparently landed on his neck which was now canted at a very unnatural angle. The detective's pale face was imbedded with cinders and Longarm knew the man had probably been dead before he struck the ground.

Before I head for the stream I had better check Upton's body to see if he has anything I can use out here, Longarm thought.

Upton did have a few useful items on his person. A sack of tobacco, cigarette paper, a small box of wooden matches and a good pocket knife. He also had about thirty dollars in his wallet and information that might be useful to send to his next of kin. Other than that there wasn't anything that Longarm needed or desired.

"You were a fool to want fame bad enough to kill a fellow law officer in cold blood," Longarm told the ruined face with its glazed over eyes. "And, for what it's worth, Upton, you probably did get a raw deal from the Army for that failed mission where your men died. But you should have put it in the past and tried to do a professional job without so much thought of what you'd get in return. A lawman's job is mostly thankless with low pay to boot. But it does have its small rewards. Pity you never figured them out."

Longarm saw Upton's hat a few feet away which he retrieved and placed over the dead man's eyes. Upton had not tumbled as far down the embankment and Longarm knew that his body would be spotted by the next passing train. The sight of Upton would bring the train to a halt and the body would be retrieved and identified. At that time Longarm hoped that he would be well enough to crawl back out of the streambed and flag help from the train. As soon as possible he would need a skillful doctor because he was pretty sure that he was still carrying a bullet inside.

He managed to climb to his feet and stagger fifty yards to the stream where Longarm collapsed beside the life-giving water to drink his fill. The water had a bitter taste and he figured it was probably tainted by alkali. But that didn't stop him from drinking because out here a man needed water or he wouldn't last very long when the heat began to build in midday.

Longarm lay on his back in the sun and closed his eyes. He reached down and touched his wound and was pleased that the handkerchief seemed to have staunched the bleeding. Now all he needed to do was to wait until a passing train spotted Upton's body. That ought to be within a day, two at the most. He thought he could last that long unless the bullet inside of him had struck a vital organ and he was bleeding internally.

In that case, he was already as good as dead.

It was midday and the sun was hot. Longarm decided to move under the train trestle in order to find shade. But when he tried to get up he found that he had grown weaker. So he crawled over to the trestle. He found that he had not been the only one who had taken shade here. A big rattlesnake was waiting under the trestle and when Longarm saw it the viper began to rattle.

"Shoot it," Longarm said to himself. " 'Cause you sure don't want to share his space."

Longarm reached for his sidearm and was upset to realize that it was missing. The Colt must have been knocked from his holster and he wanted to find it, but later when the sun was low on the western horizon. Without his gun, however, Longarm felt naked and vulnerable not only to the snake, but to anyone who might find him in his current poor condition.

The snake was still rattling hard and it showed no sign of moving so Longarm reloaded his derringer and leaned in as close as he dared. The viper really got upset. Longarm took aim with the little pistol and fired, but missed. The derringer was not a thing to use against small objects. He had a second bullet ready and he aimed and fired again this time striking the rattler just below the head. The reptile was knocked backward, its thick body half severed as it slithered deeper into the dim recesses.

"Shit!" Longarm swore, reloading the derringer from his gunbelt because it used the same caliber bullets as his Colt. He could still hear the viper rattling in the dimness under the trestle and knew that it was still capable of striking him with its deadly fangs. In his shape, he couldn't afford a snake bite on top of his existing bullet wound.

Longarm didn't quite know what to do next. He couldn't see the snake very well and doubted that he could shoot it in the head, which was what was required against such a venomous creature.

"I need to find either my six-gun or the one that Upton lost when we went over the side of that rail," he said to himself out loud.

Longarm crawled back to where he'd awakened and then began to search for a six-gun. After several minutes, he saw his own revolver half buried in the cinders and retrieved it with a sigh of relief. On an impulse he rolled Upton's body over and found the detective's weapon as well. After a moment's consideration, he decided to remove the man's gunbelt because it held about a dozen bullets. He strapped Upton's gunbelt over his own gunbelt and figured he had about thirty rounds in total.

"It'll do," he said. "It'll do until help arrives."

By the time he returned to the trestle the rattlesnake he had almost blown in half had either died or decided to move to the other side of the bridge. Longarm didn't care. He edged into the shade and rested just hoping the damned snake didn't have one last card to play and was hiding nearby ready to bite him.

He lay in the middle of the little stream feeling the warmish water flow under his body and it soothed his pain.

Longarm must have fallen asleep for several hours because when he awoke, the air was warm and he heard voices. He looked out from under the trestle and saw a band of Paiute Indians.

Longarm's breath caught in his throat. There were at least six of them and they were mounted on small, thin ponies staring down at Detective Upton's broken body. One of the Paiutes dismounted his pony to kneel beside the body and began rifling through Upton's pockets hoping to find something of value. Another of the Indians was staring at the tracks that Longarm had left when he'd crawled to shade under the trestle and pointing in that direction.

They know that I'm here, Longarm thought, *they just don't know if I'm dead or alive.*

Longarm knew that these Indians almost always were dangerous. They did not live on a reservation and they did not want white men anywhere on their ancestral lands. He also knew that they would probably want to kill him for his money, clothing, knives, guns and ammunition.

So what the hell was he to do against six of them in his poor condition? Longarm knew that he couldn't run and he couldn't hide. They could attack from both sides of the trestle and shoot into the dimness until a stray bullet killed him where he lay.

He was, in a word, trapped.

Longarm decided that the best—the only—thing he could do to save his hide was to try and negotiate with them somehow. Maybe they spoke English, but maybe not. He had to find out.

"Hello!" he called, dragging himself erect with a gun in his fist and ready to die fighting as he stood holding on to one side of the trestle for support. "I am a United States Marshal and I need your help."

The Indians grabbed their own weapons and pointed them toward him. If they chose to open fire, Longarm knew that he was going to be riddled like Swiss cheese. He just hoped they understood that he'd also take one or two with him.

"I have been shot and need your help!"

They stared at him and Longarm saw no mercy in their dark eyes. These were short, half-starved desert people who had learned to neither ask favor nor give favor to strangers—especially vulnerable white ones.

"I will pay you many American dollars," he offered. "I have money to pay you for your help."

One of the Indians, an older-looking warrior with a flat face and a red polka dot bandana on his head, detached from the others and walked forward with a rifle held at port arms. The Paiute leader didn't smile and he didn't say a word.

When the Paiute got to within about twenty feet of Longarm he finally grunted, "American dollars. You give many now!"

"Sure," Longarm told the man.

Keeping one pistol in his holster and the other in his fist he fished out the cash that he had taken from Upton's body and threw it toward the leader. The bills scattered in the air and settled on the wet rocks. A few of the bills floated on the stream to disappear under the trestle probably to be carried out the other side.

"Take it all," Longarm urged. "For your help."

The leader glanced over his shoulder at his followers who crept a little closer with their weapons, mostly old flintlocks, still trained on Longarm. Then the leader came and collected the greenbacks before he squatted for a moment to peer under the trestle searching for those that had escaped on the water.

"I need food and help," Longarm repeated. "Can one of your men go to Elko and bring me help?"

Either his request was deemed ridiculous by the warriors or else they didn't understand such a complex statement. Either way the old man shook his head. Then he said, "Guns!"

Longarm had to make a very quick choice. If he refused, there would be a fight and he would be dead meat. If he gave up the pistols, however, they might tie him up and slowly torture him. Longarm much preferred the idea of going down in a gunfight than he did trusting to the likes of this hard-looking band of roving Paiute hunters and fighters.

"No guns. I keep."

The leader's face screwed up into a fury. "Guns!" he demanded again, pointing his rifle at Longarm and then cocking the hammer.

Longarm knew that what he did next would determine whether or not he lived or died. And maybe he was crazy, but because he saw nothing of compassion or mercy in their eyes, he decided not to voluntarily give up the guns.

Not even one of them.

Instead, he raised the pistol in his hand, cocked back the

hammer and aimed at the leader's heart. Then, to add spice to what was probably going to be his last farewell, he forced himself to smile showing all of his perfect white teeth.

"No more damned guns for Indians."

The leader had not counted on this and when he saw the wounded white man grin so broadly, he was suddenly dumbfounded. His jaw dropped and his eyes widened with surprise. Then, he clamped his mouth shut so tightly that his chin almost touched the bottom of his flat nose and squinted ferociously at Longarm.

"Guns!" he demanded once more.

"Nope. Maybe today is a good day for us to die, Chief."

The leader blinked and in that instant Longarm had the vague feeling that he had won. A moment later the leader backed away and rejoined his companions. A spirited conversation took place among the group until the Indians were clearly angry as hell with each other. Longarm figured that some wanted to attack, but others thought that very unwise.

Meanwhile the sun was busting Longarm's brain. He'd lost his hat in the fall from the train and hadn't found it although it could not have been hidden very far away in the sagebrush. Longarm could now feel his head starting to spin and knew that he was very much in danger of fainting from the hot sun and the loss of blood while the Indians tried to come to an agreement about his fate.

Longarm finally eased back into the dimness under the train trestle still listening to the arguing Paiutes. They argued for more than an hour and then they mounted their poor ponies and started to ride away.

"I've done it," he whispered, feeling a tremendous sense of relief. "I've bluffed them out!"

But even as he was quietly celebrating this little victory

the Indians separated into two groups. One group stopped near a low rise on his side of the tracks and the other went over the tracks and vanished.

Longarm knew at once what they were up to. They were going to kill him in a deadly cross fire. And if that wasn't bad enough, he began to hear the now familiar and chilling warning of a rattlesnake.

In fact, as the sweat began to break out again all across his body and his blood turned cold with fear, he heard *lots* of rattlesnakes.

Chapter 9

Every fiber in Longarm's battered and bullet-riddled body told him to jump up and escape from under the trestle. Just to do it and face the Paiutes rather than remain trapped in this horrifying viper den. But when he glanced up the wash in either direction he could see shadows moving and knew the Paiutes had him cornered in this den of vipers and that there was no way out except to die in a hail of bullets.

Longarm's eyes were adjusting to the dimness under the trestle just enough that he thought he could see a rattler coiled only a few feet from his foot. He had to grip his Colt with both hands because he was shaking so badly before he fired. His bullet missed, the rattlesnake struck, but its fangs did not penetrate the thick cowhide of his boot.

Longarm fired again. The snake vanished, but that didn't stop the rest of its deadly kind from rattling even faster.

Longarm was nearly crazy with panic. He had always had a fear of vipers. When he was a boy in the South a deadly water moccasin had chased him out of a local swimming hole and nearly bit him. He'd been small then and everyone said that the bite would no doubt have been fatal. His parents and some friends had scoured the edges of the pond for hours seeking to find and kill the water moccasin, but they'd never found the poisonous viper. And Longarm had never gone swimming in that little pond or any other like it again.

Now Longarm was in one of the worst and most terrifying predicaments of his entire life. He'd rather have been standing in the sunlight facing three of the fastest gunfighters in the West than to have been trapped between the rattlesnakes and the Paiutes.

What the hell can I do!

Longarm fired several more rounds into the shadows, but the snakes weren't leaving the shade during the soaring heat of this desert day. Maybe they were thinking they'd die outside in the midday sun.

Unable to think of anything else to do Longarm edged his body into the shallow stream. He knew that snakes were not afraid of swimming, but perhaps they didn't like water being splashed in their faces. It was worth a try to find out so he holstered his gun, cupped his hand and began to hurl water and mud toward the sound of the vipers.

It was working! The rattlesnakes retreated deeper under the trestle, but only beyond the reach of his splashing.

Good, he thought, even as a Paiute bent low about fifty feet outside the trestle trying to find a target for his rifle, *it's finally my turn to inflict a little damage.*

Longarm whipped out his six-gun, took careful aim and shot the Paiute in the leg. The Indian went down yelling and Longarm could have finished him off, but chose not to. It was better, he thought, to wound as many of them as possible so that they had to leave him alone and go seek their medicine man. That's all he really wanted—to be left alone so he could crawl out from under the trestle and away from those deadly and highly agitated snakes.

The Indians now situated on both of the far sides of the trestle started firing blindly into the darkness. Longarm heard bullets whining off rocks and steel all around him and knew that he didn't stand a chance of surviving unless he dug himself a trench just as he'd done when he had been trapped on open Civil War battlefields.

He again holstered his weapon and now began cupping out mud and water and slinging it like a crazy man. He drove the rattlesnakes farther away and he didn't stop scooping and slinging until he had formed a shallow depression in the middle of the stream. A bullet nicked his ear and another clipped off the heel of his boot before he buried himself deeper almost like a salamander.

Longarm didn't return fire. He just kept his head down under the water until he needed air then he only raised his head high enough to take a gulp of air and ducked again. The bullets were screaming in around him like swarms of hornets from both directions. Once he heard a scream and knew that one of the Indians had accidentally shot another Indian on the opposite side of the trestle.

I wonder how long it will be before they come in after me, he thought. *Maybe they won't because they must have heard the rattlers. Maybe they'll get tired of wasting precious ammunition and figure me for dead.*

Longarm hoped that would be the case as he lay still in the water and prayed for an early train. Eastbound. Westbound. He didn't give a tinker's damn. He just wanted a train that would see Otis Upton's body and then the Indians. A train that would stop and drive the Indians off and then rescue his soaking, bloody carcass.

That was *all* he wanted. That and a glass of good whiskey and a doctor to pull his fat out of the frying pan along with a very bad piece of lead buried in his body.

Longarm wasn't sure how much time passed while the Indians raised hell and kept firing their weapons. However, the shooting finally stopped and he thought maybe the small band of Paiutes was leaving. But fifteen minutes later and just when he was getting hopeful Longarm saw flames and knew that they were trying to smoke him out from under the trestle.

Damn!

Being very careful not to fire too many of his remaining bullets, Longarm began to shoot at the moving shadows again in order to keep the Indians at bay. He couldn't actually see them at their work of smoking him out, but he could hear them and those damned rattlesnakes.

Then he saw flaming tumbleweeds being rolled into the openings at both ends of the trestle! Longarm reloaded his pistol thinking that he might just have to exit his unlikely sanctuary so that he could at least die like a man on his feet.

But the strange thing of it was that the smoke didn't seem too interested in going under the bridge. The Indians set up a horrific howling in their frustration. A few even dared to run down to the mouth of the opening on either end and wave blankets trying to push the smoke in on Longarm. But what little smoke did enter under the trestle stayed near the top and Longarm kept breathing clean air near stream level.

The rattlesnakes reacted to the smoke differently. Rattling even faster they slithered deeper under the bridge until they were probably all bunched up near the middle. That was fine with Longarm. In fact, if he hadn't been so weak and in pain, he would almost have found the situation a bit comical. He understood that he was in the *only* place in this entire damned desert where the Paiutes could not kill him without creeping under the trestle and risking almost certain death either by snakebite or one of Longarm's bullets.

It was, he was beginning to think, a great stroke of good fortune to find himself in this place with plenty of water and a bunch of snakes to guard his backside while he waited for help.

Dusk finally arrived and the Paiutes tried rolling some rocks down in a futile effort to trap him under the trestle. But the openings at each end were large and the rocks wouldn't pile up high enough on their own momentum to block his later chance for escape.

The Indians were furious and they shrieked at the rising moon in order to vent their overwhelming frustration. But Longarm didn't care. He just lay still in his shallow little water ditch and waited until he finally fell asleep.

He awoke once in the night and listened carefully for the sound of his enemies, but heard nothing. Quite sure that the Paiutes had finally given up trying to reach and kill him, Longarm eased out of his trench and slithered along through the water until he came to the opening. His gun was tight in his fist and he was ready to shoot anything that moved.

But nothing moved. Longarm counted the bullets left in his cartridge belt and was damned glad that he had taken Upton's extra bullets and gun. Even so, he was down to only eight shots and that wouldn't last long if the Paiutes decided to return with a new plan or some clever reinforcements.

If I leave this trestle and they catch me out there I won't survive ten minutes, he thought. *So I'd better just go back*

inside and wait for a train. To do anything else will get me
tortured and scalped.

So he crawled back to his watery little cradle and lay
still. Longarm wished he could have remained outside under the stars. He knew that the rattlesnakes were still alive
and still hiding under the trestle. Maybe they would try to
come back to their favored places near where he now lay. If
so—and he was asleep—they would sink their fangs into
his body and poison him.

Longarm kept that awful thought in his mind and it
goaded him to stay awake after midnight. But finally, his
wounds and trials overcame him and he fell asleep.

Longarm didn't know what time of day it was when he was
awakened by a faint shaking. Little pieces of dirt and rock
began to jiggle all around and then rain down on his head.
The train is coming!

He didn't know how far away the train was or even
which direction it was approaching, but none of that mat-
tered. Longarm pushed himself to his hands and knees and
began to crawl as fast as his strength allowed until he burst
outside into the blinding light of day. He shouted for help
knowing that no one on the approaching train could possibly see much less hear him.

He struggled through the hot sand and attacked the side
of the wash feeling incredibly weak. Then, he saw the
westbound train.

"Stop! Stop!" he shouted, clawing and tearing at the
sides of the wash as he fought to get up near the tracks
where he could be spotted. And failing that, Longarm
knew that at least Detective Upton's body would be seen
and that would cause the train to come to a screeching halt.

There would be dozens, maybe a hundred or more passengers and crew on the train and someone *had* to see Upton's body, wouldn't they?

But Detective Otis Upton's poor body was gone!

Longarm's head was just above the level of the wash and he could plainly see that Upton's body was missing. Oh Lordy! What . . .

The train went pounding onto the trestle. Longarm hollered at the top of his lungs, but the thundering iron wheels drowned out his weak and cracked voice.

The train just kept rolling.

And then, just as its caboose swept over the trestle, Longarm saw a railroad conductor relaxing on the back of the train smoking his pipe and taking in the scenery.

With the very last ounce of strength he possessed, Longarm raised up to his knees drew his gun and opened fire at the disappearing caboose. He was not aiming at the conductor, of course, but he wanted the man to know that the train was leaving a dying man in the wilderness.

Swaying in the warm sun, Longarm saw the conductor jump and then drop his pipe as he crouched on the platform. Longarm waved and waved. The conductor saw him! The man stared, then waved and it seemed like an eternity before Longarm heard the screech of steel on steel and knew the westbound was finally going to stop.

The entire Union Pacific train would have to back up a mile or more but Longarm didn't give a damn and was willing to wait.

In fact, he was far more than willing.

Chapter 10

Longarm felt as if he were swimming up from the bottom of a lake toward the sun. Swimming harder than he'd ever swam in his life, but he was running out of oxygen and life.

Faster, harder, he thought with his mind turning to fire in his skull. *Don't breathe, don't breathe!*

"Breathe!" the doctor's voice shouted in his face. "Don't die on me, Marshal. Breathe!"

Longarm's eyelids felt as if they were glued shut. His heart was pounding and he felt as if he were spinning off into space.

"Breathe!" the doctor yelled again, this time pinching Longarm's cheeks and then slapping his face as hard as a bartender might slap a semi-conscious drunk.

Longarm's eyes popped open and he sucked in a deep lungful of fresh air. Oh Lordy but it was sweet! All the dark clouds blew out of his mind and he stared up at the old doctor until he came into sharp focus.

"Doctor, what . . ."

"Maybe a little too much ether," the doctor explained.

"The bullet I had to dig out was very deep inside. It was a hard surgery. I couldn't risk you waking up in the middle of it so I gave you ether even though you were unconscious. Just for a moment there I was afraid I had put you into a *permanent* sleep."

"You mean killed me."

"Yes. Although you were nearly dead when the train people carried you to my office. Frankly, Marshal Long, I didn't think you would make it."

"How do you know I'm a marshal?"

"I found your badge and wallet," the doctor said as if the answer should have been obvious.

And it should have been only Longarm still wasn't thinking with much clarity. Then he remembered the fight with Detective Upton. How they'd both fired simultaneously on the platform and fallen off the train. How he'd crawled under the trestle.

And the snakes! Longarm shivered at the memory. And the Paiutes!

"It's a miracle that I'm still alive, Doc."

"You'll get no argument from me," the doctor told him. "The train people found Detective Upton. His body had been mutilated and stripped. Thrown in the brush not far from where you were found. They saw all the tracks of the Indians and their unshod ponies. How many of them were there?"

"Six."

"How on earth did you hold the Paiutes off until the westbound arrived?

"I'll tell you later," Longarm said. "But right now I must send a message to Denver on the telegraph."

"You can do that later."

"No," Longarm weakly insisted. "I need to send it *today*. Would you please take the message down on a pad and

92

use my money to pay for it? I have to get word to my boss, Marshal Billy Vail."

"Soon," the doctor said. "But first, there is someone here that needs to see you."

Longarm frowned. He did know a few women in Elko. But they could wait. What . . .

"Marshal Long!" Detective Jason Baxter blurted, hurrying past the doctor to bend over the heavily bandaged and prostrated Longarm. "We didn't think you would make it."

"So the doctor tells me," Longarm said, "but I'm a tough one to plant."

The young railroad detective's eyes jumped back and forth between the doctor and Longarm. "We didn't think you had a chance. Even Dr. Rains didn't think you'd make it when they brought you in."

"The doctor must be a fine surgeon," Longarm said, feeling very tired. "Because he saved my hide."

"Marshal, I did my best but you are the one responsible for being alive," Dr. Rains said. "Only a man with a remarkable constitution could have withstood losing so much blood and my fumbling old fingers trying to hold a scalpel and forceps. The bullet was deep. Just missed your kidney by a hair's width."

Longarm reached out and squeezed the doctor's hand. "I do owe you my life, Doctor. And I'll repay you."

"We can talk about my fee later," Dr. Rains said. "Right now, I think I'll excuse myself and let you talk with Detective Baxter. But only for a few minutes. You're still not out of the woods, so to speak."

Dr. Rains gave Baxter a hard look. "Two minutes is all I'll allow you to spend with my patient."

"Yes sir."

As soon as the doctor was gone, Baxter leaned closer to Longarm. "What happened to my partner?" he asked. "Did someone on the train murder Otis and then toss his body?"

"No," Longarm said, telling the young man the sad truth. "Detective Upton was crazed by ambition. He pulled his gun on me when I refused to step aside so that he could capture the gang all by himself. I shot him at the same time that he shot me. We fell off the train together."

Baxter's eyes widened with disbelief. "*You* shot Otis?"

"That's right. And the bullet that Dr. Rains just dug out of me belonged to your friend. Like I said, he went insane. I tried to talk to him, but Detective Upton was way beyond reason."

Jason Baxter turned away for a moment. Longarm heard the detective's long, anguished sighs. Then Baxter turned back with his eyes filled with sorrow. "I can hardly believe he'd have done that, Marshal Long. I knew Otis was obsessed with catching this gang, but . . ."

"It's finished. I'll file a complete report. But now I need someone to send a telegram to my boss in Denver telling him that I'm going to be laid up for a few days."

" 'Days?' " Baxter said with obvious skepticism. "Why I'm sure you won't be able to get up and around for weeks."

"Don't bet on that," Longarm told him. "I may not be up to snuff, but I didn't come all this way and suffer all this grief to lie in a bed while the railroad gang continues to kill and loot."

Baxter squared his shoulders. "Maybe I can at least get them identified and send for more help. Also, I've been working with the town marshal, Wyatt Dowd. He seems like he knows what's going on."

"Tell him to come by and see me as soon as he can," Longarm told the detective.

"I'll do that. We'll both come back and put our heads together on this," Baxter promised. "I'm sure that we can come up with some answers."

"Yeah," Longarm said.

"Marshal Dowd thinks that the gang is hiding right here in Nevada."

"Is that so?"

"It sure is. They hit the train just yesterday about twenty miles east of Battle Mountain. Got about eight thousand dollars."

"Did they kill anyone else?"

Baxter's expression darkened. "They shot two of our guards to death and wounded another."

"Any new descriptions that will help us?"

"Marshal Dowd says that he doesn't have any information yet. But he hopes to get some over the telegraph today."

"Ask him to find out if they were still riding those tall horses," Longarm said.

"I'll do that." Baxter managed a tired smile. "It's still hard for me to believe that Otis would draw a gun on you and go crazy."

"Well," Longarm said, "he did."

Baxter looked away and it was clear that something was very much on his mind. Longarm said, "What's eating you besides the new robbery and Upton's death?"

"I was wondering," Baxter said, "if they tortured Otis and scalped him when he was still alive."

"Neither," Longarm told the man. "Detective Upton was dead when he hit the ground because I pumped one into his heart at point blank range. And, if that wasn't enough, he broke his neck when he hit the roadbed. So he didn't suffer, if that's what's on your mind."

"He was a strange one," Baxter said. "He never much let on what he was thinking or feeling. But I thought he was . . . oh never mind."

"Upton was twisted and it had nothing to do with you but instead something that happened during the Civil War."

"Oh."

"Put the man's death behind you and start thinking about this gang," Longarm advised. "We've got our work cut out for us on this one."

"I know that and I'll carry my fair share of the work," Baxter promised. "You just tell me what to do and it's as good as done."

Instead of his help Longarm would have much preferred that Detective Baxter retire and live to grow old. The kid was as green as grass and that kind of partner could spell far more trouble than he was worth. Longarm decided to be honest with the railroad detective and not hold back. "Detective Baxter, I'm not going to tell you to back off from this but don't do anything foolish. You're young and inexperienced."

"I've had *some* experience," Baxter said defensively. "On top of that I'm smart and I'm no coward, Marshal Long."

"Never occurred to me that you were." Longarm started to feel dizzy. "Look, will you send that message to Denver? I'll give you the particulars. Have you got a pencil and some paper?"

"Sure," Baxter said, fishing them out of his coat pocket.

"All right then," Longarm said, "my message is short

and sweet. Tell Marshal Vail to send more money and that I'm down, but not out."

Longarm told the detective a little more that he wanted sent to Billy, but that was the gist of it before he closed his eyes and slept.

Chapter 11

Jim Vance was waiting for Marshal Wyatt Dowd seven miles west of Elko and he was growing more and more impatient. "Dowd said he'd meet us here at noon," Vance growled, pulling out his pocket watch for about the tenth time in the past half hour. "And he *knows* that I don't like to be kept waiting."

The man with Vance was named Grady. He was of average height, but seemed tall because he was slender and wore two inch heels. About thirty years old and with black hair and a square jaw, Grady was both handsome and well dressed. He wore a well-oiled pearl-handled Colt on his right hip and gave the impression of being very capable of using it.

Grady looked like a professional gunfighter—and was.

Grady stood beside his tall, bay gelding and said, "Marshal Dowd will be along directly, Boss. He probably got tied up with the Elko city council or maybe with that Denver marshal that you met on the train."

"Maybe," Vance conceded, consulting his watch once again. "But if Dowd wants his cut of this last train holdup, he'd damn sure better show up in the next five minutes or we're leaving. I've got to catch that next westbound at Beowawe where it takes on wood and water."

"He'll be here," Grady said and then he winked. "Why don't you just give *me* the Marshal's cut and I'll wait here to give it to him."

Vance snorted. "You'd like that wouldn't you? That would be a far easier job than killing Marshal Long in his hospital bed. But I'm not sure that I could trust you, Grady. You might decide to take Vance's share and hop the eastbound for parts unknown. After all, I've got a lot of money in my saddlebags."

"Never enough," Grady assured the leader of the train gang. "And I think we're going to be able to pull another couple of jobs before things get too hot for us to handle."

"Sure we will," Jim Vance assured his top gunny. "What I'm thinking is that we've almost done enough damage to the Union Pacific. A couple of more robberies and then we'll ride down to Yuma and start inflicting some pain on the Southern Pacific Railroad."

"Makes sense," Grady told his boss without much enthusiasm. "But it's hotter than blazes down around Yuma. And isn't there an army fort there? Dammit, Boss, I'm as game as any man, but we sure as hell don't want to take on the United States Army."

"There's a fort all right," Vance replied, "but it's a joke. Fort Yuma is an outpost for Army misfits and outcasts. It's barely manned and they don't do much except swim in the Colorado River all summer trying to keep cool. The soldiers at Fort Yuma are expected to watch over the Yuma Federal Penitentiary. Thing of it is that the guards there are almost as corrupt and worthless as their prisoners."

"Then they wouldn't give us much of a problem?"

"Not at all," Vance assured his gunfighter. "But we can talk about it later, after we do a couple more jobs on the Union Pacific."

"Why don't you tell us *where* we're going to hit them next?"

"Because you're being paid well to use those scoped rifles and to handle whatever trouble we run into on the trains. You're not being paid to second guess me, Grady. The less you and the others in our gang know about future plans the better."

"The better for you, you mean," Grady said, looking unhappy. "You're taking a third of everything. That's a pretty hefty share, Boss."

"I'm the brains of the outfit," Vance replied. "If you were as smart as I am you'd be getting a third, too."

"I'm no dummy."

"No," Vance said, quickly realizing that it was not wise to insult this dangerous gunman. "Of course you're not. And when you kill Marshal Custis Long and eliminate that threat you'll earn a bonus."

"Wonder how Marshal Long managed to fight off all those Paiutes and kill that railroad dick, Upton?"

Jim Vance pulled out his pocket watch and consulted it once again. He was really starting to get irritated with the Elko Marshal. "I neither know nor care."

Grady stroked his tall bay's neck. "I don't think you really need me to do in that Denver marshal. From what we've heard, he arrived in Elko already half dead. I guess that Upton put a slug in the marshal's belly before he died."

"Yeah, but Marshal Long is still alive and I want him dead and buried," Vance told his gunfighter. "I've met him on the train and I've done some background work on Custis Long. Everything I've learned or read about him tells me that he is extremely dangerous and difficult to kill."

"Not for me," Grady bragged.

"Don't be overconfident," Vance warned. "Even with Custis Long in a hospital bed you had better be damned careful or he'll figure a way to punch your ticket for a one way ride to boot hill."

Grady wasn't buying that and laughed. "A lot of men have tried; a lot of men have died. Marshal Custis Long won't be any different from the others. It'll be an easy job, Boss. Just don't forget the bonus you're promising."

"I never welsh on a deal, Grady. That's why I've been so successful."

"That and the fact that you sold your cattle and bought a damned gold mine up on the Comstock Lode."

"Yes," Vance said. "That too."

Grady frowned and squinted up at his boss. "Why are you into robbing trains when your gold mine is making you rich?"

"Because a man never gets rich enough," Vance said. "And also because it costs a fortune to bore into that hard rock under Virginia City. Add to that a big payroll and a lot of expensive machinery that has to be brought all the way around Cape Horn on ships. You wouldn't believe the freight costs I have to pay for some of that machinery and it keeps breaking down so I need to send more extra parts. The thing is, Grady, sometimes even a rich mine doesn't quite pay all the bills it takes to keep it in operation. So that's why I need the extra income we steal from the railroad."

Grady shook his head. "We've taken a hell of a lot of money off these trains and it's getting more dangerous with each job we pull."

"If you want big things out of life," Vance said, "you have to be willing to take big chances."

"Boss, if I had *your* money," Grady said after a few minutes of thoughtful silence, "I'd buy mining shares on the Comstock Lode that would make me even richer than you and then I'd hang up my guns and buy a whorehouse."

Grady's blue eyes filled with amusement and lost focus. "Yep, if I had your money I'd spend all day trading time between pleasuring whores and exercising a rocking chair on the porch of my mansion in Washoe Valley."

"Sure," Vance said, not believing a word of it because Grady lived to kill. "Sure you would."

"Here the Marshal of Elko finally comes," Grady said with disgust, raising a telescope that he carried in his saddlebags. "Looking just like the sorry sack of shit that he truly is."

"Don't goad Wyatt Dowd," Vance warned. "I know he doesn't look like much, but he does carry the badge."

"That's right," Grady said, with unconcealed contempt. "Dowd carries it for the highest bidder."

"What is it between you and Dowd? We're all just killers and thieves."

"The difference is that I will openly tell anyone that my gun is for hire. But your Marshal Dowd takes a regular paycheck from the people of Elko who trust him. Boss, maybe you don't see the difference, but I sure as hell do."

"Just continue to work with him," Vance ordered. "Wyatt Dowd is important to us. He's the one that learns how much money each train is carrying. And he's the one that you may need help from if something goes wrong when you try to finish off Marshal Long tonight."

"Nothing will go wrong," Grady vowed.

"How can you be sure? Marshal Long is in the hospital and it won't be that easy to reach him without witnesses."

"If anyone sees me, I'll kill them on the spot."

Vance shook his head. "I'd rather that didn't happen. What we talked about—you sneaking into the hospital and smothering the marshal—that is the way that I want it done. You need to make it look like the marshal just died of his wounds."

"What difference does it really make?" Grady demanded.

"What difference!" Vance's voice raised in anger causing his horse to dance nervously. "Don't you get it, Grady? Marshal Custis Long is a *federal* officer of the law. If it's obvious that he was murdered in his hospital bed, the feds will come down on us like stink on a skunk!"

"Even worse than they're after us now?"

"Hell yes! Right now, all we have is Custis Long. But, if he's obviously been murdered, then we'll have ten just like him arriving in Elko next week."

"All right! All right," Grady snapped as the horsemen drew near. "I'll smother the bastard."

Marshal Wyatt Dowd *did* look like a sack of shit tied to his saddle. He was a large man already going to fat although he was only thirty-one. Never a man that liked to exert himself physically, Dowd did not like horses and avoided them whenever possible. Now, however, Jim Vance had demanded this meeting and so he had been forced to ride out of town so that there was no possibility that they would be seen together.

"You're late!" Jim Vance snapped when the Elko marshal bounced up to them looking very sore and unhappy.

"Dammit, Jim," Dowd complained, "I have business to take care of in town. The mayor cornered me just as I was leaving and bent my ear for an hour. What was I supposed to do? Tell him that I had a secret meeting with you today?"

Vance decided not to say anything. Like Grady, he had zero respect for Dowd and would have preferred not to have had anything to do with the man. But the truth was that Wyatt Dowd did have his inside sources so that his information on how much money and government bonds were on each train was always accurate. Vance also knew that the railroad was sending some trains out that had no money, but extra guards hoping to capture or kill his gang. So far at least, Wyatt Dowd's inside information had kept the gang from avoiding such deadly traps.

"Let's get this meeting over with," Grady said, impatient as always.

"All right," Vance said to the Elko marshal, "when is the next train coming through this country that will be easy pickings as well as carrying a lot of money?"

"On the last day of this month," Dowd said, "there's a train coming through that will carry a small fortune in cash, gold and bonds."

Vance had a mental calendar in his head. "That's only about a week from now. April 30th is on a Saturday."

"Yep," Dowd said. "You're pretty good with dates."

"Yeah," Vance said, thinking hard. "I think we should hit this one closer to Reno."

"How close?" Grady asked. "Boss, if we hit the train too close to town, we'll have a Reno posse breathing down our necks in no time flat."

Vance had been studying his saddle horn with concentration but now he looked at both of his men. "Boys, I've got a place in mind to ambush that train that is far enough out of Reno so that we can't be overtaken by any posse."

Grady said, "But you won't tell me."

"That's right," Vance said. "Same as always. But don't worry because there definitely won't be anyone to mess us up at the place that I've picked for this next job."

"Fine," Grady said, miffed by what he considered his boss's unnecessary secrecy.

Vance turned to the marshal who was sweating and red-faced. "Grady is going to ride back to Elko, but I don't want you seen together so separate a mile or so before you reach town."

"What's Grady gonna do there?" Dowd asked, not looking at the gunfighter.

Jim Vance allowed himself a smile. "He's going to finish what Detective Upton couldn't finish."

Dowd's eyes widened. "Don't tell me he's going to *kill* Marshal Long!"

"That's exactly what I've ordered him to do, but he'll make it look as if the marshal died in his hospital bed from his earlier bullet wound."

"How the hell will he do *that*!" Dowd exploded.

"Grady will smother the federal marshal with his own pillow," Vance replied. "And your job is to make sure that Marshal Long's death receives as little notice and attention as possible."

Dowd wasn't happy. "I don't know about this, he wheedled. "There will be an investigation because he's a federal lawman and . . ."

"Shut up!" Vance barked. "Marshal Long *has* to die. He's dangerous and a loose end. He'd remember me if we ever meet and I don't want any chance of that happening."

Dowd nodded looking grim. "Anything else I need to know?"

"No." Vance reached into his saddlebags and gave the fat man a wad of cash. "Your share on this last job is almost a thousand dollars. That makes over six thousand that I've paid you since we started hitting the Union Pacific. What are you doing with all that cash?"

Dowd didn't want to talk about his money to these men so he was purposefully vague when he answered, "I'm savin' it for a rainy day."

"It almost never rains out in this country," Vance said. "You aren't putting it into a bank account like I warned you not to, are you?"

"No."

Grady smiled. "Then I guess you're hiding it in your apartment or that hog pen you call a jail, huh? Six thousand dollars is a lot of cash to be hiding."

Wyatt Dowd twisted around in his saddle and glared at the gunman. "If I ever catch you sniffing around looking for my share, I'll . . ."

"You'll what?" Grady asked with a cold stare. "Get a gun and try to kill me? Ha! Be my guest, Dowd. Against me you wouldn't last any longer than a fart in a stiff wind."

Marshal Wyatt Dowd turned to Jim Vance. "If he tries to take my money, I'll tell the authorities all that I know. Tell Grady to stay away from me, Jim. Tell it to him right now!"

Vance said to his gunfighter. "You stay away from our friend here, Wyatt Dowd. He's earned that six thousand and I don't want us to be double-crossing each other. We do that and we all go down. Understand, Grady?"

"Sure," the gunfighter said.

"All right then," Vance told them. "I'm off to catch that train. I expect to get a telegram from you tomorrow, Grady. And I expect it to say that Marshal Long died of his previous bullet wound and passed away peacefully in his hospital bed. Understood?"

"Sure, Boss."

"Oh, one thing I forgot to tell you," Dowd said. "Marshal Long sent a telegram to Denver. I managed to get a copy of it from the telegraph operator. Long was asking for some additional funds."

Vance scowled. "Did he ask for reinforcements and tell the people in Denver that he was wounded?"

"No on both counts," Dowd said. "Although I can't figure out why."

"It's because Custis Long is too proud to ask for help," Grady said. "He thinks he can break this case all by himself."

"Well," Dowd said, "that other railroad detective, young Jason Baxter, he sure wants to help him out. Detective Baxter came by to see me and he's all fired up about the case. And he said Long wants to see me right away."

Vance shook his head. "Stay away from Marshal Long. He's going to die tonight from lack of oxygen. Isn't that right, Grady?"

"Damn sure is!"

"Okay then," Vance said, looking at the corrupt Elko marshal, "just stay completely away from Marshal Long until tomorrow when you go to view his body. Is that clearly understood?"

"Sure is." Dowd expelled a deep breath. "You and Grady wouldn't hurt that young railroad detective, would you?"

"If he becomes a problem, we'll take care of him," Vance said. "You got a problem with that?"

"Well," the marshal said, looking like he was going to get ill, "he's just a kid trying to do his job. He don't know anything so he won't be a problem. I'd just hate to see a kid like that end up dead."

Vance made the decision right then and there that he would most likely have to kill this man before his conscience betrayed the entire gang. "Well," he lied, "I wouldn't worry about that, Marshal. We'll just leave him alone as long as he leaves us alone."

"Glad to hear that," Dowd said, looking relieved. "I'd better be heading back to town. People miss me when I'm gone for long."

"I'm sure that they do," Vance said. "So go along now. Grady will catch up to you in a minute."

When the Elko marshal had ridden away, Vance said, "You're going to need to get rid of him pretty soon."

"I could do both him and the federal marshal tonight, if you were to give me a double bonus."

Vance thought about that for a moment, then shook his head. "No," he decided, "wait a few days. There will be a big stir over the federal marshal's death. Let a little time pass before you take care of Dowd. Make it look like a suicide."

"What!"

"You heard me. Put his own gun to his head and blow the fool's brains out then put the gun back in his hand."

"Do you think the folks in Elko will believe he would do that to himself?"

"There will be some who won't believe Dowd shot himself," Vance answered. "But without proof, what can anyone say or do?"

"All right then," Grady said. "And I get a double bonus. Right?"

"That's right. A double bonus, but only if you get both jobs done the way I've ordered. Is that understood?"

"Sure," Grady said. "It'll be my pleasure."

"I thought as much." Grady put spurs to his horse and rode off. When he overtook Marshal Dowd he said, "I sure wish I had Jim Vance's money."

"Me too."

Grady looked at the town marshal almost with pity. "Who knows what we'll each wind up with when all the cards are finally on the table?"

Wyatt Dowd started to ask what that meant, but decided to tighten his lips and keep his mouth shut. Grady was clearly insane and it was obvious that the killer loved to use his gun.

Just the thought of going up against a gunfighter like Grady made Dowd's sizeable gut twist and lurch. He'd have to make sure that just never happened because it would be suicide.

Chapter 12

Detective Jason Baxter was extremely frustrated. He had sent Longarm's telegram to Denver as requested, but he had not been able to locate Marshal Wyatt Dowd and tell him that the wounded federal officer wanted to see him at his hospital bed.

Where could Marshal Dowd have vanished? Baxter had checked every possible place the man could have gone and had finally concluded that maybe Dowd did not want to be found for a while. But why? Baxter had narrowed it down to two reasons why the Elko marshal had suddenly vanished. Either Wyatt Dowd was in trouble or he was up to mischief, probably with a whore.

"I couldn't find Marshal Dowd anywhere," Baxter told Longarm when he returned to the little hospital where Longarm was the only patient. "The man just vanished into thin air."

"How odd," Longarm said, frowning on his hospital bed. "I wanted to talk to him right away. However, it can easily wait until tomorrow since I'm not going anyplace."

"Well, if Marshal Dowd shows up," Baxter said, "then I'll sure tell him to come right over here and visit you at once. It is kinda strange for the town marshal to just up and disappear."

"Probably with a woman," Longarm guessed. "It might be his mistress if he's married and messing around. Take my advice and don't ask Dowd when you finally locate the man. This is a small town and Dowd will eventually get his butt in a crack, if he's misbehaving or doing something on the sly."

"He just doesn't seem like the type that is going to be fooling around with women," Baxter said. "No insult intended, but Wyatt Dowd is fat and lazy."

Longarm had to smile. "Lazy or not, Jason, when a man gets lovin' on his mind it puts the lead in his pencil and he gets an itch that only a woman can scratch."

"Yeah, I guess that's true enough."

"Jason, do you have a special girlfriend?" Longarm asked. "Maybe a sweetheart you're thinking of getting married to some fine day?"

Baxter blushed. "I am sort of sweet on a girl I met in Reno. But I didn't tell her my feelings."

"Why not?"

" 'Cause I'm a lawman."

"Lawmen get married and have families."

"You didn't," Baxter said pointedly.

"I probably wouldn't have gotten married no matter what I did for a living. I might someday. But I travel a lot."

"I do too," Baxter said. "The Union Pacific sends me all over the place. A night in this town, a night in that town. Plenty of nights sleeping on the trains as they travel between Sacramento and St. Louis. But after these robberies and murders started they teamed me with Detective Upton

112

and told me to stick to him like a tick to a hound. So I did, but look what happened! Otis went crazy and you had to kill him."

"Did you learn *anything* from Detective Upton?" Longarm asked.

"I learned not to get so caught up with ambition that I lose sight of what I'm really supposed to be doing."

"That's an important lesson," Longarm said. "And there's one other you can add."

"What's that?"

"You should realize that being a lawman is a very dangerous business. Besides the danger of being killed outright, there are always strong temptations."

"Like women?" Baxter asked.

"Like women, but also like money," Longarm said. "A lawman is almost sure to be offered money for special favors. Those favors might just be simple things like taking a small bribe for looking aside when a rancher's son gets too rowdy and breaks or hurts some property or a person. Also, they can be far more serious like someone offering you a bribe to work with thieves. I've even known some lawmen that have crossed over and become hired murderers that hide behind their badges."

"Really?"

"Yes," Longarm assured the young man. "If you wear a badge long enough, you'll have all sorts of temptations."

"But I'm just a railroad detective."

"That's true," Longarm told the young man, "but you are privy to some very important inside information."

"I am?"

"You are," Longarm told the kid. "But enough of that talk. Tell me about your little Reno girl."

For the next hour and while the sun set in the West, Jason Baxter told Longarm about his love for Miss Suzy Spencer. He described her in great detail, right down to the dimples in her rosy red cheeks. It soon became obvious to Longarm that young Baxter was madly in love with Miss Spencer.

"Jason, you should tell her of your feelings before someone else does and you lose her forever," Longarm urged.

"What good would that do?" Jason asked with a sigh. "Working as a detective with the Union Pacific means I'm always gone. I only see Miss Spencer about one day a month. But even more important, I have nothing to offer her but loneliness and my pitiful paycheck."

"Then maybe," Longarm said looking the kid right in the eye, "you ought to go to Reno and discover a new line of work that pays a whole lot better and is safer."

"I'm not fit to do much," Jason confessed. "Before I went to work for the railroad and got lucky with this job, I was a swamper in a saloon and a lowly stable boy making just three dollars a week and sleeping in a stall."

"We all start out at the bottom of the rung!" Longarm countered. "And now that you're a little older I'll bet there are plenty of things you could do to make a good living. And they'd be a whole lot safer than trying to hunt down this murdering bunch."

Baxter dipped his chin in agreement. "Actually, I have been giving this job a lot of thought. But the Union Pacific has been straight up with me and I sure don't like to quit her because the going gets tough. Maybe after we land this bunch then I'll quit the railroad and find something else to do."

"That would be a very good idea," Longarm said, seeing that Jason Baxter's mind was made up on the subject for now. "But for the time being, why don't you go back and take another look around to see if you can find our missing Marshal Dowd?"

"I'll do it," Baxter said. "Marshal, can I bring you back your supper?"

"Sure." Longarm dug into his wallet and gave the young man enough money for both of them to eat well. "See you later."

"Count on it," Jason Baxter said as he left the hospital.

It was well after midnight when Grady tiptoed into Elko's small hospital and crouched in the darkest shadows for a long time listening to Longarm's soft snoring. He had his gun on his hip and he desperately wanted to just walk up to the sleeping lawman and put a lead slug in his gizzard, but Jim Vance had been very specific about how he wanted Custis Longarm's life to end.

By suffocation. *Only* by suffocation so that it would look as if Marshal Custis Long had finally succumbed to a gunshot inflicted by one Otis Upton.

Grady frowned while nervously clenching and unclenching his fists. Although he was strong, he was only five-foot-nine inches tall and weighed about one hundred and fifty pounds soaking wet. Marshal Custis Long, on the other hand, stood about six-foot-four and would easily weigh over two hundred pounds. What that meant was that the marshal had better be seriously weakened by his recent operation or Grady knew he was in for a desperate struggle. One where he could end up on the short end of the stick and drowning in deep shit.

For insurance Grady had a Bowie knife stuck under his belt. If the marshal started to really give him a fight then he'd say to hell with the boss's orders and simply slit the marshal's throat. Vance would be angry and it might even cost Grady half of his bonus, but at least he would be alive. Grady had never smothered a man with a pillow before and he wondered how long it would take even if the victim was weak.

The light was poor, but Grady had no trouble seeing the row of hospital beds. He was relieved that Custis Long was the only one on the little ward. It sure simplified things. Grabbing a pillow off of an empty bed, Grady moved as silently as a ghost on the hospital floor. He stopped beside Longarm's bed and gazed down at the federal marshal. He could see that the lawman's abdomen was heavily bandaged.

All right, he thought, *just slam the pillow down on his face and then lean on it hard. He'll likely kick and buck a bit, but the whole thing shouldn't last more than about three minutes.*

Grady reared up with the pillow and brought it down over Longarm's face. Longarm had been dreaming about a woman in Denver when he felt the assailant's crushing weight. For a moment he wasn't sure what the hell was going on. But then he tried to suck in a lungful of breath and that's when Longarm knew he was being smothered.

Longarm reached up blindly and grabbed a muscled arm. His fingers bit into flesh then inched upward to rip at a face he could not see. When he touched his enemy's jaw Longarm slipped a hand under the chin and grabbed the throat as he squeezed with every bit of his remaining strength.

Grady couldn't believe what was happening! He'd expected a strong resistance for the first minute, then less and less as the federal marshal started to lose consciousness. But he *never* expected that he might be the one to lose consciousness first.

He needed to let go of the pillow in order to keep his throat from being crushed. But, if he did that the pillow might slip away from the lawman's face. Not sure of what to do Grady felt as if his neck was caught in the talons of some giant bird of prey that was choking away his life. He heard small but vital bones pop loudly in this neck and felt terrible stabs of pain.

Grady had no choice but to let go of the pillow with one hand and try to tear Longarm's hand away from is throat. But he couldn't do it so he had to release the pillow with *both* hands.

Longarm roared with anger and fought with all of his might. For a moment that seemed to last an hour they were locked in a life and death struggle and Longarm knew that he was at a serious disadvantage because he'd lost so much strength and blood.

"Damn you!" he shouted in the dark with his words half muffled by the pillow.

Grady knew that he was losing this death struggle. The big man was still too powerful to be suffocated and his own neck was being broken one precious bone at a time.

Knife him! Get your knife out and bury it in the marshal's belly. Rip open his surgical wound and send your blade deep into his guts! And, if all else fails, pull your Colt and blast this big lawman's damned brains all over his damned bed!

Another cervical bone popped in Grady's neck and he screamed as his hand flashed to his Bowie knife. But before he could pull it out and kill the marshal, his neck bones cracked yet again and he felt hot needles shoot all the way down to the tips of his fingers paralyzing them for a moment so that he could not grip his knife.

Reeling in agony, Grady stumbled backward, tripped

over something and landed hard on the polished wood floor. Half delirious, with pain shooting into every extremity, he scrambled to his feet and then ran—before the numbness coursed throughout his entire body and he was rendered helpless.

Longarm was still on his bed and gasping for air. His gut felt on fire as he struggled to get up and go after the man who just tried to murder him. He could hear receding footsteps on the polished hardwood floor followed by the sound of a door being slammed open. But instead of getting up, Longarm collapsed back on his bed bleeding from his wound.

For long minutes he lay panting. He finally closed his eyes in the darkness and gave in to the pain and the darkness.

Chapter 13

Longarm awoke to a high-pitched scream. He opened his eyes and saw an old hospital nurse standing over him with bugged eyes and her hand clamped over her beak.

"It's all right," he assured the shocked woman. "If I'm still alive then I'll probably pull through. Go find Dr. Rains."

The old nurse turned and hurried away. Fifteen minutes later, Dr. Rains appeared looking very upset. He stared at the bloody bandage he had applied the day before and shouted, "What by all that is holy happened to you!"

"I had an unwelcome and surprise visitor last night," Longarm replied, his hand pressed on his soaked bandages. "He tried to smother me to death with a pillow, but he wasn't strong enough to do the job and that's why I'm still alive."

Dr. Rains quickly removed the bandages, all the while shaking his head and clucking his tongue with an attitude of monumental disapproval.

"I don't know how you can still be alive," he muttered.

"So much blood has been lost. You must lie very still now for at least a month. Drink lots of milk and water."

"I can't stay in bed for a month and how about me drinking great quantities of beer and whiskey?"

"Milk and water. Okay, some red wine to help build up your blood. But that is all."

Longarm was feeling pretty weak and low. He closed his eyes and said, "Doc, I know you don't like to be distracted and that you're no errand boy but I really need to see the local marshal right away. And also Detective Jason Baxter."

"No visitors today. Not tomorrow, either."

"Doc, what happened to me last night wasn't an accident or some case of mistaken identification. I *have* to see those two or the next time whoever tried to suffocate me last night will send a bigger and stronger man. If that should happen, I doubt if I could fight him off."

The doctor muttered something to the old nurse and then he finished applying a fresh bandage. "Ten minutes," he allowed. "That is all the time that I will allow you to see them today."

"Is that ten minutes *each*?"

He'd asked to lighten the doctor's mood a tad, but it didn't work. "No! Ten minutes time altogether."

Longarm didn't like being given orders even when they might be in his best interest. However, he could see by the expression of both the doctor and nurse that this was no time to argue so he just said, "I need to see those two right away."

"Ten minutes!"

"Sure, Doc."

• • •

Longarm was dozing when Jason Baxter and the town marshal appeared. They didn't look quite as upset as the doctor and his nurse had been, but they were close.

"What happened!" Detective Baxter exclaimed.

Longarm told the two men as quickly as possible. Then he said, "I managed to fight off the man who tried to smother me by grabbing his throat. He screamed. I think I either crushed his voice box or windpipe. I am certain that I injured his damned neck. You need to know that so that you can find him and arrest him. Otherwise he might try again only the next time he'll just put a bullet in me while I'm sleeping."

"Did you get a good look at him?" Marshal Dowd finally asked.

"No. It was too dark and my face was covered by the pillow for part of the time."

"Then I don't see how we can identify your attacker," Dowd said, with a shrug of his narrow shoulders.

Longarm wondered if Wyatt Dowd was as stupid and incompetent as he looked and acted. Hopefully not. "You'll identify him by the bruises I inflicted on his neck and the fact that he won't be talking with a normal voice."

"What if he's smart enough to wear a bandana around his throat and stay quiet?" Baxter asked.

Longarm scowled with exasperation. "The man who tried to smother me was wearing a pearl-handled Colt on his right hip. I did manage to catch a glimpse of the white handle during our struggle. Marshal Dowd, as I'm sure you would agree, about the only kind of man that would wear such a weapon would be a professional gunfighter."

"Yes," Dowd said, "I guess that would be true."

Longarm continued. "It is very possible that, if you find

this man, he will lead us to the ones that have been terrorizing the trains. He may be seriously injured. I know that I was sure trying to break his neck . . . and I would have if I'd have gotten both hands around his throat."

"Marshal Long," Dowd said, "I'm sorry we have to meet under these circumstances. I was going to come and visit you sooner, but I got real busy yesterday."

"Yeah," Longarm replied, "Baxter here said you were nowhere to be found all afternoon and evening."

Dowd blinked and his round face paled. Longarm figured that he had been correct and that the town marshal had been with the wrong kind of woman. He looked to see if Dowd was wearing a wedding band, but he was not. That didn't matter because the town marshal still might be a family man with a scarlet woman on the side. A lot of men didn't wear their wedding bands.

"We'll look for the man you've described and arrest him on sight," Baxter promised.

"Be careful," Longarm warned. "Such a man has to be a professional gunslinger so whatever you do, don't corner him and then force a shootout. If you do that, you'll lose."

Baxter threw up his hands. "Then what . . ."

Longarm gave Marshal Dowd a moment to jump in and tell the young railroad detective how to handle such a dangerous situation, but the marshal stayed mute so Longarm said, "What you do is to sidle up to the man and then either tackle him or pistol-whip him. If you want my advice, do the latter."

Jason Baxter nodded with immediate understanding. "You're telling me to catch him off guard before he can go for his six-gun."

"Exactly. And you can't pussyfoot around when you do it," Longarm emphasized. "Such men are suspicious by nature and always on the lookout for someone trying to arrest or kill them. So strike quick and strike hard. Give him no opportunity to get to his gun or he'll kill you in a heartbeat."

"Okay," Baxter said, nodding his head up and down rapidly. "We'll do it. Marshal?"

"Yeah," Dowd said, obviously torn from his own thoughts. "We'll go together and . . ."

"I wouldn't do that," Longarm interrupted. "If you go together, a gunfighter will be alerted right away. Maybe he will be no matter how you approach him. I don't know if he'll recognize you or not. But, if you both move in on him together it's almost a dead giveaway."

Marshal Wyatt Dowd was looking physically ill and Longarm thought he might be wrong about the man in thinking he had been frolicking in bed with a woman other than his wife. Instead, Dowd might just have been in a sick bed.

"Time!" Dr. Rains called, from the end of the hospital ward. "Ten minutes is up."

Detective Baxter looked up to see Rains rushing toward them. "What's his problem?"

"Dr. Rains thinks that I'm going to die if I talk to you men for more than ten minutes straight. What he doesn't understand is that, if you don't get this killer, he'll probably come at me again and succeed where at first he failed."

"Enough!" the doctor cried. "Go now!"

As the doctor grabbed Dowd and Baxter by the arm and started pulling them toward the exit, Longarm called out, "Find the man with a pearl-handled Colt and a stiff neck who can't talk right!"

"We will!" Baxter shouted, his promise echoing in the empty ward.

When Dr. Rains returned alone, Longarm said, "It was at least eleven minutes and I'm still alive and kickin'."

"You are not good to yourself, Marshal Long. You have no respect for your health."

"Sure I do," Custis countered. "If I didn't have any 'respect for my health' I'd have been done in a long time ago."

"Humph!" Rains snorted with disgust as he tore back the sheet to study his new bandage. Seeing no bloodstains, he turned on his heel and marched off without another word.

Longarm dozed off and on all morning and then had to force down some vile, watery soup that the nurse brought him. "Uggh!" he choked, batting the spoon away. "That stuff smells and tastes like the wrong end of a sick opossum."

The nurse's eyebrows shot up in defiance. "I cooked it myself and it's turkey soup!"

"Worst turkey I ever had to choke down. I've got enough problems already without getting the scoots. Now take that damned soup away and bring me my gun."

"Absolutely not!" she cried, spilling some of the awful soup on his clean bedsheets.

Longarm's eyes flashed. "Nurse, get me my gun or I'll get up right now and find it myself!"

The nurse was a thin old woman who was probably accustomed to bossing around all her patients. Longarm knew the type well and didn't like them, either. If you were deferential and polite and asked this type of woman in a nice manner like a gentleman then you'd never get her respect. Instead, she would walk all over you while you were bedridden and incapacitated. So you had to meet her steely eyes with your own and not back down an inch.

"Are you going to get me my Colt revolver or am I going to get up and find it?"

"You wouldn't dare!"

Longarm gritted his teeth and swung his right foot out

of the bed. He was starting to raise his left foot when the nurse shouted, "Oh, all right!"

Longarm fell back. He had to have his gun for self-defense or he was a sitting duck should the man with the pearl-handled Colt feel well enough to give him a second go.

When he had his gun once more Longarm checked the weapon just to make sure that the old harridan hadn't emptied the bullets. Satisfied it was loaded and ready to use, he slipped the six-gun under his blanket feeling much safer.

"Nurse," he roared, "I'm *still* hungry. Bring me some beef! A steak or a roast. Potatoes and gravy. Bread and wine. Lots of red wine with the doctor's full approval. And remember that I'm not going to get strong on your stinking and watery turkey soup, dammit!"

He heard the nurse respond and it didn't sound as if she was pleased with his request. In fact, it sounded like the bossy old witch was off breaking bone splints with her bare hands.

"I'll have to watch that old gal nearly as close as the man whose neck I rearranged," Longarm said to himself as he closed his eyes and waited for her to bring him some substantial victuals.

Chapter 14

Grady was sure that his neck had been cracked in at least three places. Pain continued to radiate down his spine and into every extremity. Grady could not even turn his head from one side to the other. When he tried to dip his chin, he nearly fainted and his throat was so swollen that he was deathly afraid that it would close up and he would not be able to breathe.

I need a doctor! he thought, trying to fight down his rising panic. *If I don't get a doctor's help I'm going to die. And I may die anyway!*

Fighting off waves of pain, Grady buttoned up his collar and went downstairs to discover the hotel clerk fast asleep. He saw a pad of paper and wrote: *I have a sore throat and need medical help.*

He shook the hotel clerk into wakefulness then shoved the note in his face. The clerk stared at Grady then at the note.

"There are three doctors in Elko, but only one of them is really a doctor . . . the other two just pull teeth. The real doctor's name is Rains. Mister, you don't look good at all."

Grady didn't even try to speak. Instead he dug a dollar out of his pocket and laid it down on the counter then wrote, *I'll be up in my room. Send Doc Rains to me as quick as he can come.*

"Sure," the hotel clerk said, scooping up the dollar. "Is this for me or is it a down payment for Doc Rains?"

Grady jabbed his finger into the man's chest and motioned him to move. Then, he went back upstairs to wait for Rains.

The doctor was slow in arriving and Grady was lying on his bed in his underclothes and having a tough time when the physician finally appeared.

"I understand that you've got a terrible sore throat," Dr. Rains said, coming right over to his bedside. "There's a lot of that in the spring and it can be both painful and frightening. Open your mouth and I'll have a look. You could also have a bad case of infected tonsils."

Grady already knew what the cause of his problem was and now all he needed was assurance that his throat wouldn't close down on him completely and that he would recover.

Dr. Rains said, "Open wide."

Grady opened his mouth and nearly passed out because it was so painful.

"Now," the doctor said, "say 'Ahh'!"

Grady tried to do as he'd been asked, but just couldn't. The doctor shook his head. "I don't see any sign of infection. The tonsils look normal, but your throat is almost closed. Take your hand off your neck so I can examine it, please."

Grady had been holding his throat to cover the dark bruises. For a moment, he hesitated then felt that he had no choice but to do as the doctor ordered.

"My oh my!" Rains exclaimed. "The answer to your

128

discomfort is obvious! What happened to your neck?"

Grady's mind raced and then he reached for the pencil and paper he had taken from the hotel desk and slowly wrote: *Was sleepwalking and fell in the dark on the back of a chair. Landed on my throat. Injured it bad. What can you do to help?*

The doctor got the strangest look on his face. Recovering, he said, "I recommend you get some ice and suck on it. The ice will reduce the tissue swelling. I'll tell the desk clerk to get some over at the saloon and have it brought over to you immediately. Are you in a lot of pain?"

Grady nodded.

"Can you turn your head from side to side?"

Grady forgot himself and tried to shake his head. The pain was overwhelming and he gave out a low moan.

"All right then. Don't even try. I'll go now and make sure that you get a large quantity of ice."

But Grady grabbed the doctor's sleeve and then wrote *I want opium!*

"No," the doctor said. "Opium would only make things worse. And no alcohol, either. Just lots of ice to trickle down your throat to cool and shrink the tissue swelling. Also, it will keep you from dehydrating."

Grady didn't know what dehydrating meant, but the doctor seemed competent so he allowed him to leave the bedside.

Dr. Rains stopped at the door and saw the pearl handle of a beautiful Colt revolver jutting out from a holster. Rains nodded. "I'll send a man over with ice very soon. Close your eyes and try to get some rest. I'm sure you will make a full recovery, if you haven't broken any neck bones. And I doubt that you have or you'd be paralyzed . . . although that can be a delayed condition. Just don't move."

When the door closed Grady did something that he had to do despite the doctor's orders. He eased off the bed and got his Colt and brought it back to the bed with him. Had the doctor heard the story about Marshal Long being attacked? Most likely he had. And that would mean that Dr. Rains would easily put the pieces together and realize that Grady was the one that had tried to smother Marshal Long is his hospital bed.

But what can I do to save myself now?

Grady thought about trying to get up and run away, but he just didn't think that it was physically possible. And even if he did manage to escape before the doctor returned with . . . with whom? Elko's corrupt Marshal Wyatt Dowd?

Grady relaxed. "Of course," he croaked, "my friend and partner in crime, Marshal Dowd. And it will be Elko's crooked marshal that will have to figure out some way to get me out of this fix."

And sure enough, about fifteen minutes later, Marshal Dowd and the young railroad detective burst through his hotel room with guns in their fists. Grady struggled and raised his hands so they were in full view. He croaked, "Don't shoot. I give up!"

Dowd made a big show of coming over and confiscating the pearl-handled Colt. The marshal said, "This must be the one that tried to suffocate Marshal Long at the hospital."

Jason Baxter was so excited that his gun was shaking in his fist. "Yeah, and Marshal Long says that he's probably involved with that railroad gang. I think we've had a breakthrough here, Marshal Dowd! I really do!"

Grady wanted to puke. The young railroad detective acted like he'd just arrested John Wilkes Booth after he'd assassinated President Abraham Lincoln. Grady would have laughed out in derision if he'd been physically capable. Instead, he croaked, "Ice! I need ice!"

"We'll get you ice," Dowd said, leaning close and managing a conspiratorial wink. "But first we're going to get you locked up. Can you walk?"

Grady didn't make the mistake of attempting to shake his head again. Instead, he lay quite still and let his expression tell this fool that he could hardly move.

"All right," Dowd said, finally understanding. "We'll get you on a stretcher and have you carried to my jail cell."

"Ice now!"

"Sure." Dowd turned to Baxter. "Go find a stretcher or something we can carry this man on as well as some ice. He looks to be in tough shape."

Jason Baxter nodded, his eyes hot and accusing as he stared at the man on the bed. "After what you tried to do to Marshal Long we ought to just let you choke to death. But we won't . . . and do you know why?"

Grady, of course, didn't bother to answer.

"Because Marshal Long says that you're probably one of the railroad gang and that's why you wanted him dead. You've got a lot of answers and we're going to get 'em all from you as soon as you can talk."

Grady could see the passion in the young railroad detective's eyes and hear the hatred in his voice. Grady glared back at the railroad detective and thought, *Just keep it up and I might decide to kill you too when I recover.*

Thirty minutes later Grady was lying in a clean jail cell on a straw mattress that wasn't all that much worse than the hotel bed he'd been lifted from. His neck was still a torment, but the tingling had left his hands and feet and now he was sucking furiously on ice, confident that he would live another day.

"I'm going to go over to the hospital and tell Marshal Long that we have the man who tried to kill him last night," Baxter said, almost dancing because of his excitement. "He might have some instructions for us before we interrogate our prisoner. I'll be back as soon as I can."

"Take your time, Detective Baxter," the marshal said. "I'm not going anywhere and neither is our prisoner."

"All right then," Baxter said, hurrying off.

The moment that they were alone Marshal Dowd came to stand over Grady. "Well, Grady," the marshal said looking down without a trace of compassion, "you sure messed things up royally for us. You were supposed to kill Marshal Long, but now he's in far better shape than you are."

Grady signaled to the fool that he wanted to write something down on paper. Dowd went to his desk and returned with writing materials and watched as Grady wrote *In a few days I will be able to kill the federal marshal. Just keep your mouth shut and everything will be fine.*

"We're supposed to do another job in five days near Reno and I can't even get ahold of the boss," Dowd whined.

He doesn't need to know. Don't panic and don't give anything away about the next job. I'll be okay soon.

Dowd shook his head with frustration and it was clear that he was very nervous and upset. "Easy for you to say. But I'm the one that has to hold everything together because of your failure."

Right at that moment, had he been physically capable of the act, Grady would have loved to have killed this stupid and weak local marshal. Instead, he said nothing, but he knew that he was going to kill Dowd and then Marshal Long.

Grady knew that it wasn't a question of *if*, it was only a question of *when*.

Chapter 15

Longarm was more than pleased when Detective Baxter rushed into the little hospital ward with the news that his attacker had been arrested and locked up in the Elko jail.

"Nice work!" he exclaimed.

Detective Baxter shrugged and grinned. "Shoot, it was Doc Rains who should get all the credit. He recognized the killer and sent for us right away. He'd be here right now telling you all about it except that he had to rush out of town to deliver a baby. But I'm sure he'll be back tonight and then he can tell you all the details. Old Doc, he's a cool one, all right."

"I'll look forward to hearing it from him," Longarm said. "I just wish that I could come over to the jail and talk to the prisoner right now. I really am convinced he tried to kill me because he's part of the railroad gang."

"You must have injured his neck pretty bad," Baxter said. "The man can barely speak and he can barely move his head."

"I sure wish I could see him today. But Doc Rains

would kill me if I moved over to the jail," Longarm said, "so I guess that means that my talk with him will have to wait. I can't take a chance of reopening my wound and losing any more blood."

"I could be your go-between," Baxter offered. "You could tell me your questions and I could ask them to our prisoner and come back here with the answers."

"It might be worth a try," Longarm said, rather doubtful that young Baxter would be able to get the prisoner to talk. "All right, ask the man what his name is and where he came from."

Baxter frowned. "Don't you want me to ask him why he tried to smother you with a pillow?"

"Not yet. Besides, I already know the answer. It has everything to do with the railroad gang. They didn't want me on the case."

"Are you sure I shouldn't ask him who's the leader of the gang and when are they going to strike the Union Pacific next?"

"Don't do that," Longarm said decisively. "If you asked him those questions either he'd clam up completely or give you false information. Just ask him his name and where he's from. And don't be disappointed if he refuses to say anything. We'll just keep after him with the simple questions until I get over there."

"Sure enough," Baxter said, looking a bit disappointed.

"Is Marshal Dowd trying to get anything out of the prisoner?" Longarm asked.

"I don't know. I haven't seen him asking the man any questions. He mostly just seems to even avoid looking at him."

"How strange," Longarm said. "But that's fine. I'd rather everyone wait until I can be there."

"Sure," Baxter said. "Anything else?"

"Yeah, send out some telegrams and see if any of the town marshals along the U.P. line have seen and remembered our jailbird."

"Good idea," Baxter said, brightening.

"And keep me posted," Longarm called.

"Will do!"

When the young detective was gone the old nurse appeared. "The doctor specifically said to me that he didn't want you to have a bunch of visitors. You're supposed to lie still and quiet."

Longarm glared at her. "Nurse, what's for dinner?"

"Ham and potatoes."

"Good," Longarm said. "The sooner I eat again the better. And bring me plenty of wine to go with it. I'd prefer it to be a well-aged French wine, not that sour red vinegar you brought the last time and called a port."

"This isn't some fancy hotel where you can order people around, Marshal Long. This is a *hospital*."

"Well," Longarm said, "what you need are more patients. Some that you can buffalo and boss around."

The nurse's mouth twisted up like a dried prune. "I don't like you, Marshal. I don't like you a bit!"

"The feeling is mutual. How about bringing me some wine before dinner?"

"Humph!" she snorted and marched off.

Longarm grinned. The news he'd just received about the capture of his would-be assassin really was terrific. He just wished that he could get out of this bed and go over to the jail right now. By damned he would get some answers out of that prisoner in a helluva hurry. But that would be stupid. And like Detective Baxter said, their prisoner wasn't going anywhere in the next day or two.

"If I could go over there right now I'd grab him by the throat again and wring it like a chicken!"

The gunfighter Grady looked at the young detective and said in a whisper, "Boy, I ain't tellin' you my name or where I'm from or any damn thing you want to know so leave me alone."

"I checked that tall horse that you boarded at Clancy's Stable," Baxter said, hoping to catch this bloody bastard off guard. "Really a fine-looking animal. I'll bet he can run real fast after you rob trains."

"I don't know what the devil you are talking about," Grady hissed. "Why don't you go and change your diapers or something?"

Baxter's face flushed with anger. "I'm probably about as old as you and I won't take being insulted!"

"Yeah, well what are you going to do about it then?" Grady taunted. "Are you going to come in here and beat me up when I can barely move?"

"I think you can move one helluva lot better than you let on," Baxter told the prisoner. "And I also know that you're one of the train robbers. Right now you're being treated with kid gloves, but when Marshal Long gets out of the hospital in a day or two he's going to come over here and make you sing like a yellow canary."

"Get lost, boy. You're boring me."

"I'm going to telegraph up and down the line with your description. I'll bet someone knows your name and where you're from," Baxter threatened, watching for some sign that he had finally shaken this man's cocky defiance.

But Grady just sneered. "Go ahead and waste your time and money on telegrams."

"I wish I could come in there and strangle you myself!"

"Ha! Even in as bad a shape as I am right now I'd kill you quicker than you could spit," Grady bragged, his mouth twisting down in contempt. "Boy, you're way out of your league when it comes to taking on a man like me."

Baxter bit back a reply. He had nothing more to say so he went off to send messages. If this man was indeed a professional gunfighter, it seemed likely that someone up and down the railroad line would have seen and remembered him. Because, like Longarm said, there just weren't a lot of men running around wearing pearl-handled revolvers on their hips.

Chapter 16

Two days later, Grady was napping on a warmish afternoon when Detective Baxter again brought up the telegrams.

"Get lost, boy," Grady said with irritation because he'd been dreaming of a hot loving Cajun woman in New Orleans.

But Baxter ignored the insult and was looking very pleased with himself. "I sent all those telegrams out on you and guess what?"

Grady said nothing because he could well guess what Baxter was about to say next.

"Since you're not talking I might as well tell you what I found out. I just now received a telegram from the sheriff in Reno and he says that you murdered two men in cold blood and that you're a wanted man. They've put a reward on your head of three hundred dollars alive—or dead."

Baxter waited for Grady to say something and was disappointed by his silence.

"Well, Grady?"

"You're boring me, boy."

"We'll see how bored you are when they march you up a gallows in Reno."

Grady didn't give the kid any satisfaction. And besides he was feeling much better. His neck was still sore and the bones in it creaked when he turned his head too fast, but the tingling in his fingers and toes had finally subsided. He wasn't yet his old self, but Grady was able to function again and that meant using his six-gun when he got it back.

"Haven't you got anything to say about Reno?"

"Sure I do. That Reno sheriff is full of crap," Grady said, sitting up on his jail cot. "I never killed anyone in Reno. Hell, I haven't even been there in six or seven years."

"That's not what the man is telling us in his telegram," Baxter said. "Anyway, he's coming on the first train he can catch in order to pick you up and take you back to Reno. The man says that it's certain you will dance at the end of their hangman's rope."

Grady came to his feet and moved over to the jail door. "You'd like that, wouldn't you, Detective?"

"Sure," Baxter said. "I've known that you were a killer right from the start. You've probably gunned down quite a few innocent train passengers and employees. And you know what, Grady? I'm going to Reno to watch you hang and to collect that three-hundred-dollar reward! I sent back a second telegram to Reno saying that I would be accompanying the sheriff just to protect my reward money. I'm sure that will suit the sheriff just fine and I'll enjoy watching you sweat on the ride to Reno."

Grady couldn't stand to watch the kid gloat and so he turned around and went back to his cot and lay down with his face to the wall.

"Sweet dreams, Grady. You're finally going to pay the piper."

"Get out of here!"

"I'm going right now," Baxter said. "Going to find Marshal Dowd and tell him this latest good news. Also, I'm going to go to the hospital and tell Marshal Long that we know who you are and what you've done. I'm sure he'll want to come right over here first thing tomorrow morning and interview you before that sheriff from Reno arrives. And I'll bet he beats some answers out of you. Yes sir, mark my words that big Denver lawman will have you singing like a yellow canary."

Grady swore savagely as the door shut and he was left alone locked in his cell. Baxter's news was the worst possible. He *had* killed a couple of cowboys in Reno and then hastily beat it out of town just before a lynch mob would have stretched his neck. That being the case, there was absolutely no doubt that he would be hanged in that town.

Even more immediate, however, was the threat of Marshal Custis Long coming to interview him in the morning. Grady knew that Long would probably empty the office so there would be no witnesses and then he'd proceed to beat him to a bloody pulp. Just the thought of Marshal Long twisting his neck made Grady half sick to his stomach.

"I've got to get out of here," he muttered to himself. "I've got to get out before Long and that Reno sheriff arrive."

Grady stared up at the ceiling of his little cell and thought about his sad predicament. A few minutes later he turned his head to look over at the fly-specked calendar that Wyatt Dowd kept on a nearby wall. Let's see, today was Wednesday, April 27th so that meant there were only three more full days until Saturday's planned train holdup east of Reno.

"I've got to get out of here *tonight*," Grady decided out loud. "Just as soon as it gets dark. Otherwise I won't be in on this last train job and I won't get any money from it."

Grady lay still on his cot for more than an hour trying to decide how he would get out of jail and then get to Reno in time to be a part of the April 30th train robbery. It was almost three hundred hard desert miles between Reno and where he was now and Grady knew that he would never be able to ride a horse that far given his bad neck. And a stagecoach would be too slow and almost as punishing as a horse. That meant he needed to catch the westbound Union Pacific train first thing tomorrow morning. It would deliver him to Reno late tomorrow night or the next morning and that would give him ample time to find Jim Vance.

Now, all he had to do was escape this jail and quickly get out of Elko.

At about eight o'clock that evening Marshal Wyatt Dowd finally appeared carrying a tray of food. Grady noticed that the marshal was unsteady on his feet and he could smell his whiskey-soaked breath.

"Evening," Dowd said, not looking at his prisoner as he placed the tray of food on his cluttered desk. "Sorry I'm a little late, but I had some business that I had to attend to."

"Did you send a telegram to the boss telling him our situation?" Grady asked.

"Nope. In the first place it would be too risky. In the second place I don't know who would deliver it to Mr. Vance."

"I have to get out of here," Grady said, skipping right to the subject of most importance. "I'll jump the train tomorrow morning east of town and tell the boss about what happened here myself."

Dowd's jaw dropped an inch. "Oh," he said, "you can't do anything like that!"

"Sure I can."

Dowd came over to the cell. "Grady, you know that if I let you escape I'd lose my job."

"So what! You've made enough money off these train robberies to retire for life. You're not worth a damn as a town marshal anyway. If you stayed, sooner or later someone like me would gun you down. It's a break for you, Dowd. Take the money you've got hidden and run."

Dowd went over to his desk and sat down to think. But being as he was half drunk that wasn't too easy. He kept shaking his head and finally Grady got mad and shouted, "Dammit, at least bring me my food while it's still warm!"

The marshal nodded looking almost relieved to do something other than to consider the hard choice that his prisoner had just offered. He unlocked the cell and then turned to go back to his desk to get Grady's supper tray.

Grady slipped out of his jail cell right behind the man and when they reached the desk he snatched Dowd's six-gun out of his holster and pistol-whipped the town marshal before he could even shout in alarm.

"Oh, gawd, why'd you go and do that to me?" Dowd whined. "You hurt my head real bad, Grady!"

Grady ignored the man and went over to his desk where he knew that his pearl-handled Colt and Bowie knife were to be found. He holstered his gun and knelt beside the prostrated marshal with the Bowie knife clenched in his fist.

"Dowd," he said, looking into the man's watery, blood-shot eyes, "you are about the sorriest town marshal I've ever come across and I've seen some real pathetic ones. You, however, take the prize."

Wyatt Dowd didn't care about hurt feelings right at that moment. "What are you going to do now?"

"Depends."

"Depends on *what*!"

Grady gave the marshal his coldest and most chilling smile and Dowd actually shivered in fear. "Depends on how fast you tell me where you've hidden your share of the train robbery money."

"No!" Dowd cried. "It's *my* money. I've earned it!"

Grady leaned over the marshal and placed the Bowie knife under his sweating jowls. "I want your share now. Tell me where you've hidden it or I'll slit your throat."

Big, wet tears welled up in Marshal Dowd's eyes and slid down his bloated cheeks. "Oh, please. It's all I've got in this world. Don't take it all, Grady. Please don't do this!"

"All right," Grady said, pulling the blade back an inch. "I'll split it even with you. That way there should be over three thousand for each of us."

Dowd swallowed hard and even tried to strike a better deal. "I'll give you a thousand if you'll just let me alone. Take your gun and I'll even get your horse and bring it around behind the jail. You can ride out of here tonight and be halfway to Reno a thousand dollars richer."

"Fifty-fifty," Grady insisted, placing the knife back against the marshal's fat neck. "Say yes or no. But, if you say no, that's the last thing you'll ever say in this world."

"Yes!" Dowd sobbed.

Grady pulled the knife from its leather sheath and said, "Then let's go to your place and get the cash right now. Get up and move! I haven't got time to mess around with you, Dowd."

"It's hidden *here*," Dowd blurted.

"Here in this office?" Grady couldn't believe this piece of good fortune.

"Yes. I wouldn't be stupid enough to leave it in my room where the cleaning woman or someone else could find it. It's right here practically under our feet!"

"Better yet," Dowd said, slipping the Bowie knife into its leather sheath and then turning his Colt on the man. "Show it to me."

"Fifty-fifty? Right? I'm still valuable. I can stay here as town marshal and we can keep robbing Union Pacific trains. I'm the only one that has a source that can tell us what they're carrying. Right, Grady?"

The man was desperate and so pitiable that he almost made Grady want to puke. Apparently he'd forgotten that the boss had said that they were riding south to take on the Southern Pacific in order to escape the increasing pressure from lawmen. "Sure. Fifty-fifty. Now shut up and show me the cash."

Grady climbed to his feet and hurried over to his desk. He gave it a hard shove and the desk moved about six inches. Even with blood leaking out of his scalp and running down into his collar, Dowd managed a triumphant smile. "I kept it hidden under this floorboard that one leg of my desk was resting on. Pretty smart, huh?"

Grady said nothing as the sheriff produced a pocket knife and then proceeded to pry up a small piece of the wooden floor. He watched with growing anticipation as Marshal Dowd reached down under the floor and pulled up a handsome black leather satchel.

"Here it is," Dowd said, holding up the satchel. "It holds exactly six thousand four hundred and twenty dollars."

"Put it on your desk and divide it up as I watch," Grady ordered. "I don't want you to cheat me."

"Oh, I wouldn't do that!"

"I'm sure, but count it out anyway."

Dowd dumped all the cash on his desk and then in an almost singsong voice, he began to count the money as he separated it into two equal piles.

When the counting was done the fat marshal started to say something over his shoulder. But whatever it was, Wyatt Dowd never finished because Grady drew his Bowie knife, stepped up to Dowd's broad back, reached over the man's humped shoulder and slit his hog-fat throat.

Blood gushed out of Dowd and would have sprayed across his desk and the two piles of cash if Grady hadn't shoved him sideways to the floor. And as the dying town marshal gasped and wheezed through his severed windpipe, Grady scooped up the lovely bills and replaced them in the fine leather satchel.

"So long, Dowd! Have a nice day in hell!"

He took a rifle and the marshal's coat and hat which were both too large but concealed his identity well enough to get him out of town in the darkness. Finally, he confiscated the keys to the jail and its cell. On his way out Grady locked the outside office door and then he went to collect his horse. He would gently ride the tall animal west all night and hail the train somewhere out in the desert tomorrow morning. By then, people might or might not be trying to break into their marshal's locked office.

It didn't matter. Grady knew that he would catch the train a far richer man. He wouldn't even tell their boss Jim Vance what he had done until after he received his bonuses and this last job was finished.

After that, Grady thought he might quit the gang. The idea of riding all the way down to Yuma in May where it was already hotter than blazes just didn't suit his fancy. Instead, perhaps he'd take his small fortune and head for New Orleans where the ladies were especially fine to a man of means and the food and liquor were simply out of this world.

Chapter 17

That next morning Longarm joined Detective Baxter and slipped out of the hospital while the nurse and Dr. Rains were absent. Longarm wasn't feeling quite up to snuff, but he was doing just fine. He'd received enough wounds in his life to know that he was healing nicely and that only a direct blow to the wound would cause it to resume hemorrhaging.

"Grady is his name," Baxter was saying as they moved along toward the marshal's office.

"First name or last?" Longarm asked.

"No one seems to know. But I did get some additional information from Reno in a second telegram that just might interest you."

"Go on."

"The telegram said that Grady had been known to stay at a cattle ranch in Washoe Valley."

Longarm stopped in mid-stride. "Did you say *Washoe Valley*?"

"Yeah. It's between . . ."

"I know where it is," Longarm said. "Halfway between Carson City and Reno. Did the telegram say the *name* of the cattle ranch or its owner?"

"Yeah. The ranch is called the Circle V."

"Sonofabitch," Longarm whispered in amazement. "I was snookered!"

"What do you mean?"

"I met the owner of the Circle V Ranch on the train out of Cheyenne. His name was . . ." Longarm had to think hard for a moment to remember. "Ranch," he mused, "rhymes with . . . Vance! That's it. The man was real smooth and his name was Jim Vance."

"And you think . . ."

"I know," Longarm said, cutting off the detective. "It's too unique a circumstance to be a coincidence. Jim Vance was on that train to find out my plans and then alert Grady of my whereabouts so he could kill me."

"You told him you were a United States Marshal?"

"No," Longarm said, "I told him that I was a gambler. But I remember Vance saying I looked more like a businessman or a lawman. He knew that I was a lawman and he was just having his little fun. He played me like a fish on the hook and all the while I thought he was a heck of a nice fella."

Longarm stewed on this new information as they made their way to the marshal's office. It wasn't often that he could be snookered any more by anyone. But Vance had been exceptionally smooth and he'd pulled it off with a smile. That was enough to make Longarm's blood boil.

When they reached the marshal's office his door was locked. Longarm looked to his young friend. "Do you have a key?"

Baxter rifled though all of his pockets and came up empty. "I do, but I guess I left it back at my hotel room."

Longarm was more than impatient. "Pound on the door and shout. Maybe Marshal Dowd is still sound asleep."

"This late in the morning?"

"Who knows," Longarm said dryly. "He might have been up half the night rousting drunks out of saloons or carousing with a painted lady. It doesn't matter so long as I get inside and have some time to talk to Grady. Now that I know the name of the man he works for perhaps he'll be more willing to talk."

"I doubt it," Baxter said. "Given that he's a candidate for the gallows over in Reno."

"Make some noise and let's find out," Longarm ordered.

Detective Baxter pounded on the marshal's heavy wooden door until his hand hurt and he shouted, too. But still there was no response and that was surprising. "You'd think," Longarm said, "that at least Grady would shout back at us from his jail cell. Baxter, go around in the alley and see if you can peer through the jail bars into the cell and office. Something isn't right here and we need to find out what it is fast."

"Yes sir!"

Longarm remained by the front door while Baxter ran around in back. The detective returned in less than three minutes and he was as pale as the belly of a carp.

"What is it?"

Baxter shook his head. "The jail cell door is open and I saw a large pool of blood over by the marshal's desk."

"*His* blood?"

"I don't know. There were a pair of feet I could just barely see sticking out in view, but I couldn't see who they belong to."

"They have to be Marshal Dowd's feet," Longarm said, his voice tense. "Go get your key to this door. It's too stout to kick open."

Again, Baxter sprinted down the street while Longarm paced back and forth in front of the office. Several passersby stopped and bid him a good morning, but Longarm was barely able to act civil.

Finally Baxter returned, unlocked the door and they burst inside to see the bloody carnage. The young detective sat down heavily in an office chair. Longarm just shook his head and then said, "I know you're tired of running, Jason, but you'd better go find the mayor and the undertaker."

"What are you going to do?"

"I'm thinking," Longarm said. "Where was Grady's tall horse stabled at?"

"Clancy's Stable. It's just up the street a block."

"That's where I'm going."

"You think that Grady got his horse and rode off this morning?"

"No," Longarm said, toeing the wide pour of blood that had drained from the marshal's slit throat and had coagulated into a dark, almost rust color. "I think he got his tall horse and rode off *last night*."

"But the gunfighter was in no shape to ride very far."

Longarm turned on the young detective. "One of the worst mistakes a lawman can ever make is to underestimate the opposition. And I'll tell you something. Grady wasn't a big man, but he was very strong and he was facing a noose. Given those facts I'll bet he could ride to hell and back if he had to in order to save his hide. Wouldn't you agree?"

Baxter grimly nodded his head. "Grady swore he'd kill me if we ever met again."

"Then I'd damn sure better catch or kill him first."

"I'm going with you," Baxter said.

"You would be better off staying here."

"No! You're wounded and I'm a lawman. So I'm going and I won't let you talk me out of it."

"All right," Longarm replied as he hurried off to Clancy's Stable. "Then bring your guns and keep your mouth shut when I need to think or act."

"Yes sir."

When Longarm reached the stable a few minutes later Clancy O'Toole was pitching hay to horses and not looking very happy with the world. Longarm got right to the point. "I'm looking for the tall horse that Marshal Dowd's prisoner owned."

"You're about twelve hours too late," Clancy said, leaning his pitchfork up against his dilapidated barn. "The horse was stolen last night. Not only the horse, but one of my boarder's saddles. It was almost new and worth forty dollars. Guess who will have to pay for that?"

"You will," Longarm said. "Unless I catch that prisoner."

"I didn't even get paid for the animal's board yet. I've got to remind Marshal Dowd again that I'm owed . . ."

"Marshal Dowd was murdered by the prisoner last night," Longarm told the Irishman who then swore a blue streak when he heard this additional bit of bad news.

"How on earth is a man supposed to stay in business in this damned town!" Clancy ended up yelling. "I make practically nothin' and now this!"

"I'm sorry," Longarm said without any more sympathy than Clancy had shown over the death of the town's marshal. "But now I need a horse."

Clancy glared at him. "You were shot and taken in the hospital, right?"

"That's right."

"Did you pay your hospital bill . . . or are you goin' to stiff me and them both, if I rent you a horse?"

"Listen," Longarm said. "I will pay you *cash in advance.* But I need an easy rider because my bullet wound isn't completely healed. No rough riding horse? Understand?"

"Sure. But I've got nothing here that would catch that tall thoroughbred that was stolen last night. Not even catch the trail of his dust."

"I'll worry about that."

"Fine," Clancy said, "then show me cash and you can take your pick of my horses."

"You pick the horse that rides easiest and will go the distance," Longarm told the Irishman. "I'll be back in twenty minutes. Oh, and you'd better saddle another of your best horses for Detective Baxter."

"You payin' for *both* animals in advance? Be a hundred dollars even."

Longarm dug out the money and paid the man. "You'll rent us your best horses or I won't even bother to return that boarder's new stolen saddle," Longarm warned.

Clancy carefully counted the money. Satisfied, he asked, "You and that kid going after the marshal's killer?"

"That's right."

"If it's any help he rode west. I saw his tracks. Followed them out into the street where they was buried by wheel tracks and those of other horses. But at least from here to the street your prisoner was going west."

"Following the railroad line?"

"Maybe so," Clancy said, looking over at the train yard and the tracks stretching off into the hazy gray desert horizon.

"I'll be right back," Longarm told the Irishman as he

hurried off to get his rifle and gear. He really wasn't up to a hard chase on horseback, but he'd do what he had to do. Longarm just hoped that young Baxter wasn't going to add to the trouble and misery that he was already about to endure.

Chapter 18

Grady saw the train coming from the east and he had to push his tall sorrel to its very limits on a long uphill grade. His racehorse was nearly out of wind when Grady came even with the caboose. He was an expert rider and it wasn't much trouble for him to jump from his flagging mount onto the back platform of the Union Pacific.

"What the hell!" said the conductor who had watched Grady as he'd come flying out of the sagebrush to catch his train. "What are you doing, man!"

"I'm catching this train to Reno," Grady said as he slapped the dust off his clothes and took a deep breath.

"What about your horse!"

Grady looked back with genuine regret at the thoroughbred that was probably worth five hundred dollars. And he sighed with additional regret thinking about the new saddle that he'd have loved to keep. But then he turned his back on them and said to the conductor, "I've got almost a hundred dollars on me and it's yours if I can stay in this caboose all the way to Reno without anyone knowing I'm on board."

"That's impossible," the conductor, a man in his early fifties, snapped. "Passengers have to buy tickets at the stations and then they ride in our passenger coaches. This caboose is off limits to anyone but myself on this run."

"In that case," Grady said, "you're about to have a *very* bad day."

His hand flashed upward with his gun and he said, "Jump or I'll put a bullet in your brain. Doesn't matter to me either way."

"But . . ."

"This train isn't moving fast, mister. You'll most likely land without breaking bones. Better than having your brains splattered, isn't it?"

"But it's twenty-five miles back to Elko and I'll die of thirst, if the Paiutes don't catch and scalp me first."

"Life is tough, ain't it?" Grady said with a smile as he raised his gun, cocked back the hammer and aimed to shoot the man between his eyes.

The conductor dove off the train. He struck the side of the roadbed in a cloud of dust and cinders then went rolling down a steep slope to vanish into the heavy sagebrush.

"He must have been smarter than he looked," Grady said to himself as he holstered his pearl-handled Colt and went into the caboose to relax and find out what there was to eat and drink.

Sandwiches and water. It wasn't great fare, but Grady wasn't complaining. He had his own private car in addition to a place to stretch out and sleep during the long, hot miles. Even better was the fact that he was free and on his comfortable way to Reno.

• • •

At midmorning, Longarm and Baxter found Grady's tall sorrel horse running loose. It was covered with dried sweat and walking back toward Elko.

"What do you think?" Baxter said, catching up the thoroughbred.

Longarm removed his hat. It was warm and there wasn't a hint of a breeze to cool down man or beast. "I'm thinking one of two things must have happened. Either Grady is hurt worse than we thought and fell off someplace ahead, or else he caught the westbound and had no choice but to leave this valuable horse and saddle."

"I hope it's the first option you mentioned," Baxter said. "If he's caught the train then he's gotten away from us."

"That's what I was thinking," Longarm said, his eyes on the western horizon. "Let's take the sorrel along and keep riding west as fast as we can. That's the only way I know of to find out what happened."

Around noon, Longarm and Baxter saw a man standing by the tracks waving a white handkerchief and favoring one leg.

"Now who do you think that is?" Baxter asked as they spurred their rented horses up a long grade.

"Someone who works for your boss," Longarm replied. "Someone who is very lucky just to be alive."

When they reached the battered conductor they dismounted and gave the poor man water from their canteen. His name was Sam Milner and Baxter knew him well.

"He was going to blow my brains out unless I jumped . . . so I jumped! Fortunately, the train wasn't moving fast, but I landed wrong and wrenched my knee real bad. It won't take my weight."

"Can you ride?" Longarm asked the man.

"Sure can."

Longarm dismounted and handed the reins over to the conductor then helped him up into the saddle. "Detective Baxter, hurry back to Elko and wire the marshal in Reno that Grady is on the westbound. Conductor, does that westbound train stop anyplace for the night between here and Reno?"

"No. But it takes on wood and water at Beowawe."

"Any other stops?"

"Yes," the conductor said. "It makes another stop at Battle Mountain which is only another twenty-five miles."

"For how long?"

The conductor's brow furrowed. "There was a flash flood that took out a trestle just before you get to Battle Mountain. We have a full repair crew working on it, but I'd say that it won't be passable for quite some time."

"Meaning how long?" Longarm asked impatiently.

"Between waiting for the trestle repair and the stop they have to make at Battle Mountain, they won't be leaving at least until this evening."

Longarm looked at Baxter. "I'm taking the fast horse. Maybe I can catch that train."

"But you're not in any condition to ride that far and hard!"

"I'll do the best that I can," Longarm said, lengthening the tall sorrel's stirrups to fit his own legs. He also transferred his rifle to the sorrel.

"Can't I come along?" Baxter pleaded.

"No," Longarm said. "Take Mr. Milner back to Elko and send that telegram to Reno. Then catch the next train you can to Reno where we'll hook up and take Jim Vance into custody."

Longarm didn't wait to hear any more arguments.

Time was of the essence and he had some hard miles ahead of him.

Longarm was two hours behind the train when he got to the water tank and woodpile at Beowawe. His sorrel had given him a tremendous effort, but now it was shot and staggering.

"I need a fresh horse to get me where that trestle crew is working," he told a railroad foreman as he showed the man his federal officer's badge. "There's a killer on board that westbound train."

"There are two company horses in the corral," the foreman said without any hesitation. "The buckskin is far and away the better animal."

The foreman looked down at Longarm's side and saw the heavy bandaging under his shirt. "I'll switch your saddle, blanket and bridle. Marshal, do you have time to let me check that bandage and to eat?"

"Afraid not. Just give me something to take along and eat in the saddle," Longarm replied.

Ten minutes later, Longarm waved goodbye to the small crew at Beowawe and galloped off on the buckskin. It was a raw and rough riding animal, but Longarm sensed that it was also powerful and in great condition. So he just rode the buckskin beast for all it was worth.

Twenty-five more miles? Is that what the conductor had told him it was between Beowawe and that washed out trestle? Why, he could do that. Hell yes he could if it meant getting his hands once more around Grady's neck!

Chapter 19

Longarm saw a trail of smoke rising into the vast empti-
ness about two miles and he hoped it was the train repair
crew cooking their supper rather than a band of Paiutes up
to some kind of troublemaking. Not sure of which he
would find he continued to ride hard until he was about a
mile from the smoke and then he dismounted. Tying his
horse to a bush he rushed up to a brushy hill that would
serve as a good observation point.

To his relief, Longarm saw the repair crew and the westbound train. The unfortunate part was that the U.P. locomotive was puffing smoke and looking as if it were getting
the steam pressure up in its boilers.

"That means that the trestle repairs are about finished
and the train is getting ready to roll," he said to himself.

Longarm hurried back to his exhausted horse whose
head was hanging low and whose coat was covered with
sweat and foam.

"We're almost there," he told the buckskin as he remounted and forced it back into a jolting gallop. "Not far now."

The buckskin had served him very well and he felt sorry for how hard he had pushed the animal since leaving Beowawe. But now the man who had tried to smother Longarm and who had slit Marshal Dowd's throat was almost within his grasp.

As Longarm thundered through the sage he could see that dozens of passengers who had been allowed to get off the train to stretch their legs and breathe fresh air were now all being called back to their seats.

"Come on!" Longarm cried, urging the powerful buckskin to its maximum effort. "We're almost there!"

The train blasted its steam whistle three times and Longarm saw the last visible crewman wave goodbye to the repair crew and then hop on board. Longarm was still half a mile from the train and a sense of despair set in as he began to think that he would not be able to reach the train before it gathered full speed and left him far behind. Then he realized that the train had to climb a small grade beyond the trestle and that the tracks bent back in his direction. Making a quick decision to leave the tracks and cut across the rough country, Longarm reined the buckskin in even heavier brush and let it beat its way through in order to shorten their angle and intercept the train.

His gamble paid off and they broke out of a low ravine to discover that they were intersecting the middle of the train. Longarm had no idea which passenger coach Grady would be in, but he suspected it would be the caboose where he had attacked the conductor and made him jump. So he whipped his buckskin up to the closest platform hoping he would not fall and either be severed by the train's wheels or have his bullet wound torn open.

His hands grabbed the railing and he jumped wishing that he could take his rifle with him but knowing that he needed both hands to have any chance of making this dangerous transfer.

Longarm made it! He half fell onto the platform between two passenger cars and lay there gasping for air as he had been the one running all those rugged miles instead of the buckskin. He looked back at the horse which had veered away from the train and was now standing straddle-legged with its head down gasping for breath.

"Thanks!" Longarm said in a quiet voice as the horse suddenly laid down. Longarm didn't know if the valiant animal had burst its heart or if it was simply too weak to stand at the moment. He hoped that it was the latter and supposed he'd find out one way or the other—if he survived Grady and the rest of the railroad gang.

Passengers and crew who had witnessed his startling appearance now came to help.

"I'm all right," Longarm said, climbing to his feet and inspecting his bandages which showed no signs of fresh blood.

"What's going on here?" a uniformed porter asked.

"I'm a United States Marshal. Would you please ask your passengers to return to their seats? I need to speak to you in private."

The porter was a man in his mid-thirties and looked both capable and intelligent. "Can I see your badge, Marshal?"

Longarm fished it out of his pocket. Satisfied, the porter ushered the passengers back into their traveling coaches and then he returned. "What's going on?"

"There's a killer on board this westbound and he's part of the gang that has been robbing Union Pacific trains. He's a gunfighter. Very dangerous. I *have* to find and arrest him before we get to Reno."

The porter nodded with understanding. "I'll help you in any way I can, Marshal. What does this man look like?"

"Average height. Slender and he wears a pearl-handled Colt on his right hip. Other than that, I can't tell you anything because I only saw him myself for a moment in the darkness when he made an attempt on my life. Oh, but he would have bruises on his neck so you'd either see them or he'd have them covered up with a bandana."

The porter shook his head. "I serve every passenger on board and there isn't anyone that fits that description."

Longarm frowned. "Are you absolutely sure?"

"Yes."

"Then he must be somewhere other than the passenger coaches. In fact, I'm quite sure that he is probably still in the caboose. Have you seen your conductor, Mr. Samuel Milner lately?"

"As a matter of fact, I have not. I was about to go look in the caboose to see if he'd taken ill."

"Your conductor was tossed off this train by a killer named Grady." Longarm brushed off his clothes and checked his gun. "I expect that is where Grady is still hiding."

"You say that Mr. Milner was thrown off this train?" The porter was clearly shocked.

"Well, actually he said that he had to jump or else he'd have been shot to death," Longarm explained. "But don't worry, other than a badly twisted knee, your conductor is just fine and in safe hands."

"Thank heavens! What can I do to help you, Marshal? Naturally, my main concern is passenger safety."

"I understand. Is there a car where there are men guarding the safe or valuables being carried on this train?"

"Yes. It is four cars to the rear."

"If you'll escort me there I'll have a quick word with the

guards and try to come up with some plan. Grady would be far more valuable to me alive rather than dead. He knows the names and probably the whereabouts of all the members of the train gang and I'm sure they're gathering right now to hit this line hard again. If they do that, they'll not hesitate to kill more crew and passengers."

"I understand. Follow me," the porter said.

When Longarm entered the security coach, two nervous-looking guards nearly jumped out of their skins. "Nobody is supposed to be in here except us," a huge man shouted over the hammering of the train. "What is wrong here?"

Longarm took charge and after showing them his federal officer's badge he quickly explained what he was doing on the train and what yet needed to be done in the hope of taking Grady alive.

"I'll need one of you men to climb up on top of the caboose as quietly as you can and then go along the roof to the back."

"You mean while it's moving?" the big Pole who said his last name was Budzenski asked.

"Yes. There must be handrails or something to hang onto up top."

"Sure, but . . ."

"Budzenski, if you do as I ask and help me take this man alive, I can force him to tell us who is in the gang that has murdered many of your fellow crew members as well as passengers. And, if you *both* help me, I'll personally see that you're given equal credit and very favorable recognition from the government as well as your employer. I'm sure that would result in some kind of bonus or promotion from the Union Pacific Railroad. Now, are you going to help me capture this killer or not?"

"All right," Budzenski agreed. "I'll go on top."

"Good," Longarm said. He looked to the much younger guard who was clearly scared and therefore could not be counted upon to play any major role in this attempt to capture a seasoned gunfighter like Grady. "Young man, I want you to stay close behind me. If I take a bullet and go down when I enter that caboose, you're going to have to do your best to shoot to kill. Failing that, keep Grady pinned in the caboose. Is that understood?"

"Yes," the younger guard replied, taking up his rifle.

"The idea," Longarm said, "is that Budzenski goes over the top of the car and then drops down on the back platform and causes a distraction."

"What if the gunfighter comes out on the platform to shoot me?" the Pole asked.

"Jump."

The Pole's lantern jaw dropped. "Jump?"

"That's what your conductor did and it saved his life," Longarm explained. "I just need you to distract Grady for a second so that I can enter the caboose and get the drop on him."

"Will he stand to be taken alive?"

"I don't know," Longarm said honestly. "But I'm a good shot and I might be able to wound him and still get the information that we need."

The two guards exchanged glances and then Budzenski said to his underling, "You back this marshal up if he falls. Don't run away like a coward."

"I won't. I promise."

Longarm could see that both men were extremely worried and it seemed to him that the best thing he could do was to get his plan into immediate action rather than letting the pair stew and think about what they were about to do next.

"All right, Budzenski. Up on top and across to the back of the caboose."

"But Marshal," the Pole exclaimed. "How will you know . . ."

"I'll be at the front door of the caboose watching through the little window. When I see Grady start to move toward you I'll jump in and order him to drop his gun or take a bullet in the back."

The big Pole nodded with understanding yet obviously not with complete confidence in Longarm's daring plan of action. But then, hell, Longarm wasn't too confident of the outcome himself. He only knew that he had to take whatever risk that was necessary to try and capture Grady—and failing that, to put a stop to the cold-blooded murderer once and for all.

Chapter 20

Longarm crouched just under the little pane of window in the front of the caboose and peeked inside to see if Grady was awake or asleep. The man was asleep, but even as Longarm watched he saw the gunfighter jump off the small bunk and stare at the caboose's ceiling with anger and alarm. And then Grady drew his six-gun and began firing right up through the roof.

Longarm was appalled. What if one of Grady's wild bullets actually struck and killed the big Pole? In that instant, Longarm knew that there was nothing to do but to stop Grady from doing any more shooting. He cocked back the hammer of his Colt and jumped into the caboose.

"Freeze, you're under arrest!"

Grady swung around and fired all in one fluid motion. Longarm fired at the same instant from a crouched position. Grady's bullet shattered the little pane door window, but Longarm's slug caught Grady in the upper part of his chest and right lung. The gunfighter staggered backward, braced himself and fired once more at a distance of less

169

than ten feet, but the hammer of his pearl-handled Colt struck on an empty.

"Damn you!" Grady gasped as he slid down to the floor with bright red blood pumping onto the front of his shirt.

Longarm hurried over to the man and frisked him to make sure that he had no second gun. He tossed the Bowie knife aside although he was sure that Grady didn't have enough strength left to use it. Satisfied, Longarm sat back on his heels and studied Grady who had closed his eyes and was failing fast.

"You're dying," Longarm told the man. "Tell me what you can before you die so that no more innocent people are killed in this next train robbery."

Grady's eyes popped open and he glared at Longarm. Then he cracked a smile and he croaked, "Yeah, you punched my one-way ticket. But I'm no songbird. No canary. What's in it for me, lawman?"

"I'll notify your relatives of your death. Maybe they'll give you a real burial instead of you getting planted in a pauper's grave with no headstone and only a cheap wooden cross bearing your name."

Grady looked down at the blood spurting through his shirt with each dying beat of his heart. "Lawman, I only got a sister. I'm carrying over six thousand dollars in that leather satchel. Give it *all* to her."

"No deal. It's train robbery money so I can't do that."

"She's sickly and alone!" Grady's eyes flashed with rage. "Damn you, then give her a thousand and I'll talk. Otherwise . . ."

Grady began to cough up blood and couldn't finish his sentence.

"All right," Longarm said. "I'll see what I can do about

giving your sister a thousand dollars. Where does she live and what's her name?"

One agonizing word at a time, Grady choked, coughed and spit blood while he gave Longarm the name of a Mary Higgins who lived in Reno.

"I'll do what I can for her."

"Do I have your word on that, lawman?"

"Yeah."

Grady nodded and then smiled as he made a joke. "Lawman, if I had a Bible I'd have you swear on it. But I just happened to have lost my Bible about twenty years ago."

"You're dying! Tell me who is behind these train robberies. Is it Jim Vance?"

"Yeah," Grady whispered.

"When and where is his next attack coming?"

Grady's whole body began to shake in his last mortal moments. "Saturday."

"This Saturday?"

"Yep."

"Where?"

"Twenty or thirty miles east of Reno."

Longarm grabbed Grady's arm and shook the man back into awareness, "Grady, I need to know *exactly* where and when they'll strike the train."

But Grady's chin drooped down to rest on his bloody chest. "Don't . . . know exactly," he whispered. And then, for just a moment, the glaze over his eyes cleared and he cried, "Lawman, you'd better give my sister that gawdamn money!"

"I'll help her, Grady."

The gunfighter shuddered, his boot heels danced on the

floor of the caboose as Longarm heard a death rattle in his throat. At the same time, both Budzenski and his young partner burst into the caboose with their guns cocked and ready to fire.

"Easy! Don't shoot!" Longarm called, afraid that the two inexperienced men might kill him by mistake in their extreme excitement.

They lowered their guns and Longarm climbed to his feet. He saw a handsome leather satchel on the bunk and he knew it would contain a lot of stolen railroad cash. Longarm picked up the satchel and started for the door just as the train was slowing into Battle Mountain.

"What should we do with him?" the younger man asked, his face twitching with shock.

"Grady's body is going all the way to Reno," Longarm told the guards. "He has a sister there. She's his only relative, probably the only one on earth he gave a damn about. Maybe she even loved him in return."

"He nearly killed me up on the roof," Budzenski said, shaking his head with wonder and peering up at the splintered ceiling. "I don't know how he could have shot so close to where I was crouched."

"He was a real professional," Longarm answered. "I shouldn't have let you take that chance on the roof, but if I hadn't I would probably be dead instead of Grady."

Budzenski nodded with understanding. "Marshal, I hate to ask this right now, but will you still give us a letter of recommendation? We both could use a promotion or a pay raise."

"And you'll deserve one," Longarm told them. "I'll write the letters just as soon as I take care of the last of this deadly business."

The big Pole and his young helper smiled with gratitude. Then Budzenski said, "I don't like to see so much blood and a dead body. We don't have to stay here with him, do we?"

"No," Longarm said. "Just make sure that no one comes in and robs or disturbs the body until the undertaker can collect it in Reno."

With that finished Longarm took the satchel and headed into the passenger cars. He didn't want to talk to anyone although he could tell by the looks he was getting from both the passengers and crew that everyone wanted to talk to him. Longarm just needed a little time to sleep and to be left completely alone because he suddenly felt very tired. Despite the blood and death he'd seen these last two days, Longarm was satisfied because he was about to come to a showdown with Jim Vance and his ruthless gang.

He'd need help, of course, and he hoped to get plenty of that when he arrived in Reno. But most likely young Detective Baxter would not arrive in time to take part in the showdown. Probably just as well. Although the kid was game, he was too nice and needed to find a new profession and marry his sweetheart before he was shot and killed by a man like Grady.

Minutes later, Longarm with the bulging black satchel tight in his fist found a seat off by himself. After the train took on wood and water in Battle Mountain it was only about two hundred empty miles to Reno.

And considering what he'd done and been through, two hundred miles was just a walk in the park.

Chapter 21

When the train pulled into Reno at about five o'clock on Friday afternoon, Longarm gave instructions that Grady's body was to be taken to an undertaker and that he was to have a proper—not a pauper's—burial.

"What do you care how he's buried?" Budzenski asked. "He almost killed us both."

"I promised Grady a proper burial and that's what he's getting," Longarm answered. "Will you make sure my instructions are followed?"

"Who's payin' for it?"

Longarm dug fifty dollars out of his pocket. "This ought to do it. If it costs more, look me up."

"Where?"

"Damned if I know," Longarm said, walking away from the confused Pole.

He went straight to the marshal's office and told him everything except about the money in the satchel. Longarm couldn't keep that stolen money but he wasn't quite sure he wanted to turn it all back to the railroad. He'd think about it later after he'd had time to count it and find Grady's ill sister.

Marshal Tom Nolan was a quiet man in his forties with pale blue eyes and a handlebar mustache who seemed competent and determined to do whatever was necessary in order to eliminate the train robbers once and for all.

"If you're pretty sure that they're going to strike tomorrow then we have damn little time to get some men together and set a trap."

"I know that," Longarm said. "And I'm sorry that I couldn't get this news to you sooner, but I've been pretty tied up."

Nolan's eyes dropped to the bulge under Longarm's shirt. "Bandaging?"

"Yeah."

"You okay to do this?"

"Sure," Longarm said. "Can you get about ten good riflemen collected in time to help out on this?"

Nolan steepled his long fingers. "I can get twenty men that can shoot."

"I'd rather have ten," Longarm told the Reno marshal. "And I'd like them to be unmarried."

"Sounds like you think this is going to be a rough outing."

"It will be," Longarm told the man. "These boys we're going to face have everything figured out. Tall, fast horses and even a few of them with telescopic sights on their rifles."

"Then why not more men?"

"Because it's critical that this is done with secrecy," Longarm told the man. "If we try to get twenty men, the odds double that one of them will inform on us and tip off Jim Vance and his men. Then, we'd be back to square one. Also, ten really good shooters can be every bit as effective as twenty men blasting away."

"It's your show," Nolan said. "I'll get the ten men gathered. Then what?"

"Swear them to secrecy. Tell them that there will probably be reward money that they can share but that there will be real danger. If any of them are expert marksmen and have telescopic rifles, tell them to be ready to use them tomorrow."

"How are we going to do this if we don't know the exact time or place that the robbers are going to hit the train?"

Longarm had put a lot of thought to that very question. If he had been able to get that precise information from Grady before the gunfighter died, it would have made things far easier. They could have set up a trap and caught the robbers in cross fire, some of them being on the train and some hiding in the brush. But since they didn't know the exact place where the attack would come they would all have to be on board the train.

"What time does the eastbound leave here tomorrow morning?"

"Eight-ten."

"Are they usually on time?"

"Never more than a minute or two off," Nolan assured him.

"Then we'll be on that train. Some in passenger cars but most in baggage and the security car. When the robbers attack the train, we'll wait until they've dismounted and I'll order them to throw down their guns."

"Do you really think those murderers will do it?"

"Not a chance," Longarm said. "But I have to ask before we start swapping lead."

"I understand. Otherwise, we'd be murdering them just like they've been murdering the train's crew and passengers."

"That's right," Longarm said. "So go about your business and pick us ten good fighters who can shoot straight and not panic under fire. Have them meet us here tomorrow morning at about four o'clock."

"In the dark?"

"Yes," Longarm said. "We need to all sneak on board the train before the crews or passengers arrive."

"But they'll see us before the train pulls out."

"I know that," Longarm said. "So what we have to make sure of is that nobody that boards and sees us hiding can get off the train. That way, there is no chance that Vance can possibly be tipped off that we have set a trap for him and his gang."

"You've thought this out pretty well," Nolan said.

"I had a lot of time to think it out between here and Battle Mountain. Marshal Nolan, we're just going to get one good shot at this bunch of thieves and murderers so we can't afford to ruin the opportunity. That's why you have to pick men that not only can fight, but will keep their mouths shut."

"I understand that. When I pick 'em I'll have them come directly to this office and spend their time until four o'clock tomorrow morning. That way, they will be stone cold sober and have no chance to make a mistake in a saloon this evening."

"Good idea," Longarm said, appreciating the man's suggestion. "On quite another subject, do you know a woman living here named Miss Mary Higgins?"

Nolan's stern expression softened. "*Everyone* in town knows Miss Higgins. She's a living saint in Reno because she does so much charity work through her church and several other organizations."

"I understand that she is not at all in good health."

"I'm afraid that's correct. Mary has tuberculosis. The

doctor says she needs to go south where the sun shines more, the winters are easy and it's much warmer. He says that will improve her breathing and extend her life. But Mary is pretty stubborn and besides she hasn't any money to get started over down South. She lives at various church members' homes and is poorer than a church mouse."

"Where can I find her?"

"Our Presbyterian Church is just two blocks off Virginia Street. Big stone building. You can't miss it."

"Thanks," Longarm said as he headed out the door.

"Say, what's Miss Higgins got to do with anything?"

"I just need to pay her a visit about a brother. You see, I shot him to death on the train coming in and she needs to know about it and take charge of his funeral."

"Oh." Nolan shook his head. "Do you want me to tag along for support?"

"No," Longarm told the man. "Just get your best shooters together. Get them ready for what I expect will be a tough fight because Jim Vance and his boys know they'll hang if they surrender."

"I'll do 'er," Nolan promised.

Longarm found the Presbyterian Church and came upon Mary Higgins tending to an old woman who was in poor health and whose eyesight was almost gone because of thick cataracts.

Longarm had removed his Stetson when he entered the church and now he whispered, "Miss Higgins, my name is Custis Long. I'm a Deputy United States Marshal out of Denver and I need to speak with you for a few moments in private."

"About what?" the frail but quite beautiful young woman asked.

Longarm studied her face for a moment. Mary looked almost angelic. It was nearly impossible to believe that the murdering gunfighter Grady was her brother.

"About your brother?"

Mary's eyes clouded with worry. "Is he all right?"

"Could we step outside and talk alone?"

"Of course."

Mary told the old woman that she would return in only a few moments and that there was nothing to worry about. Once they were outside in the sunshine, Longarm could see that Mary's skin was as white as bone china and that she weighed no more than a hundred pounds despite the fact that she was rather tall.

Longarm didn't know quite how to begin to break this sad news and his sudden anxiety must have been evident because Mary placed her hand on his arm and said, "Grady is finally at peace, isn't he?"

"Yes he is."

"Did you . . ."

"Yes."

Longarm was carrying the black leather satchel. He'd never counted the money and he'd avoided doing so on purpose although he didn't understand that purpose until this moment.

"There is some money in this bag. Quite a bit, I think."

Mary's eyes dropped to the satchel that he extended to her. "It's from my brother?"

"Yes. He wanted you to have it."

"I can't do that. It is probably stolen money."

"I'm not sure," Longarm said, willing to tell the small lie. "But as he was dying I promised him that I would deliver it to you and that he would receive a decent Christian burial."

Her eyes brightened and the sadness was momentarily swept away. "Did Grady ask for a Christian burial?"

Longarm couldn't help himself and said, "Yes, Mary, he did." It was a much bigger lie, of course, but the instant he told it Longarm could see an immense burden seem to lift from this kind and beautiful young woman's thin shoulders. "Mary, your brother said that you should have this money to do good for yourself and for others."

Tears filled her eyes and dripped down on the satchel. "All right," she said after a long deliberation. "I'll use it for good works. And thank you."

"You're welcome."

She reached out and touched the bandages under his shirt. "You've been wounded. Did my brother . . ."

"No," Longarm said quickly. "Your brother had nothing to do with this wound."

"I'm so glad."

"Me too," Longarm said, thinking about how her brother had tried to smother him to death and had slit Marshal Dowd's throat from ear to ear. But he would never tell Mary Higgins of those horrible acts.

Never in a thousand years.

"Goodbye," Longarm said. "I hope you use some of that money to travel south where it is warmer and dryer so that your lungs will heal."

"Someone told you about that? Perhaps my brother before he died?"

Longarm just nodded his head and walked away. At the end of the block, he saw that Mary Higgins had gone back into the church to help the blind woman.

"I did the right thing," Longarm said to himself. "Too bad that the Union Pacific Railroad will never know how proud it should be of itself today."

Chapter 22

"Here they come!" Longarm whispered as Jim Vance charged the train followed by almost a dozen men on tall horses. In addition to Vance Longarm spotted a giant on a powerful bay horse and he was galloping hard alongside a midget on a beautiful dapple gray.

"Don't anyone move or shoot until I order them to surrender," Longarm said one more time as they crouched in the baggage and security car. He and Marshal Nolan had also positioned a few of their best sharpshooters in the caboose and the locomotive. They each had telescopes on their hunting rifles.

The railroad gang had struck farther out in the desert than Longarm had expected. This desolate place was where the stinking Humbodlt River finally gave up its flow and was swallowed by the hot desert sands. For miles around there was just a barren salt and alkali plain where not even sagebrush could survive.

The moment the attack on the Union Pacific train began Vance started to fire his six-gun into the sky as a signal and his riders peeled off into three groups. One bunch rode hard for the locomotive where they would order the engineer to apply his brakes—or die. Another bunch headed toward Longarm and the vault while the third spread out to rob the passengers. As he watched them attack, Longarm could not help but admire the gang's military-like coordination and precision.

The train began to slow just as Longarm had ordered. Then, as Vance drew his horse up and jumped to the ground along with most of his gang, Longarm stepped into view.

"Freeze, Vance! You and your men are under—"

Longarm didn't have time to finish. Jim Vance had already been holding a gun in his fists and now he opened fire. Longarm returned fire and he could suddenly hear the booming of many big hunting rifles.

Vance and most of his gang were instantly cut down in a hail of bullets. Some of the outlaws fell fighting and others were dead before they struck the railroad bed. Longarm saw two of the gang's deadly sharpshooters standing on a low rise and taking careful aim. The little circles of their telescopes glinted in the harsh desert sunlight as they fired. But within seconds both of the marksmen crashed over backward as Marshal Nolan's hand-picked sharpshooters found the range and drilled their counterparts.

Jim Vance was trying desperately to urge the last of his gang to retreat. The trouble was that they had all dismounted and now their high-strung thoroughbreds were rearing and jumping around in confusion and terror. A chestnut was accidentally shot and pinned its half-mounted rider to the earth. The outlaw's leg was trapped and probably broken, but he continued to shoot until a bullet struck him in the face and blew it away.

The giant was an easy target, but he took at least six bullets before he toppled like a huge oak tree. His murderous little friend took off running fast through the brush because his dapple had escaped. A sharpshooter positioned at the locomotive blew a hole in the little killer's back and sent him tumbling down a hill in a shower of loose rock and gravel.

Jim Vance was badly wounded, but still trying to mount his horse when Longarm jumped off the train, raised his gun and shot the man twice in the back. Vance fell and his foot slipped through the stirrup causing his thoroughbred to drag him down the tracks as if he were a swinging rag doll. Vance's head struck the rails over and over and sounded like eggs cracking against a skillet. The terrified racehorse veered off into a wash and vanished but they could still hear the pounding of its hooves and Vance's head as it struck rocks.

And then as suddenly as it had begun the firing was over except for two or three scattered shots from the marksmen who saw an outlaw or two twitching or still trying to lift their guns.

Longarm walked over to the giant and used the toe of his boot to tip the man's face up to the hot sun. Marshal Nolan came over to join him. They both watched as the other racehorses went chasing after the one that was still dragging the body of Jim Vance.

"Those horses won't last out here if we don't find 'em and get them to good water."

"They're valuable and you'd better go round them up," Longarm said, watching the alkali dust boil into the sky.

"I take it that was Jim Vance that the first horse dragged off?"

"Yeah."

Nolan sighed. "Vance should have stuck with raising horses and cattle."

"He fooled me once," Longarm said, holstering his weapon, "but I'd be damned if I let him fool me twice."

Nolan watched the last thoroughbred disappear. "This is one helluva bad place to meet your end," he mused aloud.

"*Anyplace* is bad to meet your end," Longarm answered, thinking about Miss Mary Higgins and wondering if she would take that money and go find a warm and drier place to extend her sweet life.

Probably not, he decided. So maybe he'd go back to Reno and make absolutely sure that she got her chance in the southern desert. Yeah, he'd do that for sure because saints on earth like Mary were just all too good to let die young.

Watch for

LONGARM AND THE RESTLESS REDHEAD

the 329th novel in the exciting LONGARM
series from Jove

Coming in April!

Explore the exciting Old West with one of the men who made it wild!

**AVAILABLE WHEREVER BOOKS ARE SOLD OR AT
PENGUIN.COM**

(Ad # B112)